CW00746369

Into the Storm

Amanda Wills

Copyright © 2015 Amanda Wills
All rights reserved. No part of this publication may be
reproduced, stored in a retrieval system, or transmitted, in any
form or by any other means, without the prior written
permission of the author, nor be otherwise circulated in any
form of binding or cover other than that in which it is published
and without a similar condition being imposed on the purchaser.
This book is a work of fiction. Any resemblance to actual
persons, living or dead, is purely coincidental.
ISBN: 1511638389
ISBN-13: 978-1511638388

To Sue and David McDine, for their unerring encouragement and support. And for always having faith in my scribbling.

CHAPTER 1

The sun was already peeping over the horizon when Poppy McKeever tugged open her curtains, her heart as heavy as a millstone. Vapour trails criss-crossed the tangerine orange sky and the flute-like warbles of song thrushes and blackbirds rang around the old stone cottage on the edge of the moor. There wasn't a breath of wind. It was going to be another beautiful day. But Poppy felt numb.

She opened her window, looked down at the stable below and whistled softly. A loud heehaw drowned out the birdsong and two noses appeared over the wooden door. The first was brown and hairy, the colour of milk chocolate. It belonged to Chester, the donkey she'd inherited when they'd moved to Riverdale. The second was silver grey. Cloud pushed his handsome head over the stable door and looked up. He saw Poppy's pale face framed in the window and whickered. She blinked back tears, rubbed an impatient hand across her eyes and eased the window closed.

A muffled buzz made her jump. She'd forgotten she'd set her alarm for the crack of dawn and had shoved the clock under her pillows so the ringing didn't wake everyone. It had been a complete waste of time. She'd barely slept. She'd spent most of the night staring, hollow-eyed, at the ceiling.

Silence restored, Poppy headed for the landing, trying her best to ignore the packed holdall in front of the wardrobe. She'd gone to bed in her jodhpurs and a long-sleeved tee-shirt so she didn't have to squander even a few minutes of the precious time she had left getting dressed.

Chester had pushed Cloud out of the way by the time she reached their stable. Poppy scratched the donkey's wide forehead and he nibbled the zip of her fleece. She darted into the tack room, returning with Cloud's saddle and bridle. The leather gleamed in the early morning sun. Poppy had spent hours the night before cleaning his tack when she should have been packing. But she had wanted everything to be perfect for their last ride.

Cloud stood calmly as she ran a body brush over his dappled grey summer coat. The Connemara was muscled and fit, a far cry from the skeletal, blood-stained pony she had watched stumble around the sale ring the previous autumn. She sniffed loudly. As if sensing her distress Cloud turned his head and

2

nuzzled her hair.

"We'll ride up to the top of the tor and watch the sunrise," Poppy told him. Chester watched with solemn eyes as she sprang into the saddle and turned her pony towards the gate that led to the moor.

Excited by the prospect of an early morning ride, Cloud danced through the gateposts and up the stony track that meandered lazily around the base of the tor. Poppy squeezed the reins, coaxing him into a walk.

"Soon," she promised him.

They skirted the Riverdale wood, passing a small herd of Dartmoor ponies. A chestnut mare with a skewbald foal at foot looked up and whinnied. Cloud arched his neck and snorted back. Soon the olive-green slope of the tor lay before them, as inviting as a racetrack. Poppy gathered her reins and clicked her tongue. Cloud picked up a canter, his neat grey ears pricked. Poppy urged him faster and he lengthened his stride into a gallop. She didn't need to guide him. After living wild on the moor for so long Cloud was as sure-footed as the native ponies and he raced nimbly past boulders and tussocks, never putting a foot wrong.

By the time they reached the top of the tor there was colour in Poppy's cheeks and a light sheen of sweat on Cloud's neck. She slid off him, flung her arms around his neck and finally let the tears fall.

"Oh Cloud, I'm going to miss you so much," she gulped. He regarded her calmly with his beautiful brown eyes. Poppy buried her face in his mane and sobbed noisily as the sun rose in the forget-me-not blue sky behind her.

Charlie was swinging on the stable door by the time they arrived back at the cottage. He took one look at Poppy's tear-stained face and his eyes widened.

"What's happened?"

"Nothing." Poppy felt drained. The last thing she needed was an interrogation from her seven-year-old brother. She jumped down and led Cloud towards his stable.

"Shall I get Mum?"

"No!" she snapped. "I'm fine. Cloud's fine. We're. Both. Fine."

"Well, you look like you've been crying to me," he pressed.

Poppy glared at Charlie. She knew she'd get no peace until she told him what was wrong. "I was upset because I don't want to say goodbye to Cloud, if you must know."

"Upset? Why?"

"Why do you think? I don't want to leave him."

Charlie was quiet as he watched Poppy untack her pony. You'd have thought from the tragic look on her face that someone had died. He couldn't understand it. She'd been so excited when she'd found out.

"Poppy -" he ventured.

"What now?" She spun around and shot him a look that would have sent a lesser soul scurrying for cover. Their dad had always advised him against reasoning with emotional women, but Charlie was nothing if not tenacious. He took a deep breath.

"I don't understand what all the fuss is about. You're only going for *five days*."

OK, so she probably was over-reacting, Poppy reflected as she flung her holdall into the boot of their car and waved goodbye to Charlie and her stepmum Caroline. But she was going to miss Cloud like crazy. She caught her dad's eye in the rear-view mirror as they bumped down the Riverdale drive.

"All set?" he asked.

"I guess so."

"I thought you were looking forward to this holiday?"

Poppy had been, but now she wasn't so sure. "Look, there's Scarlett," she said, changing the subject.

Her best friend was waiting at the bottom of the drive, perched on a tan leather suitcase that looked like a relic from the turn of the century.

"Great case, Scarlett. Is it vintage?" asked Poppy's dad, as he heaved it into the boot.

Scarlett cackled. "No, just ancient! We never go on holiday and it was the only case Mum could find. It smells of lavender and mothballs, so I think it must have been my granny's. I'm so excited. I didn't sleep a wink last night," Scarlett grinned as she slid into the seat beside Poppy.

"Me neither," said Poppy, her grey mood lifted

marginally by the sight of Scarlett's freckled face and her best friend's infectious enthusiasm.

"I wonder what the ponies will be like. I hope I get something a bit fizzy." Scarlett's Dartmoor pony Blaze was a safe, steady ride and no amount of oats made a difference to her even temperament.

"I wish I could have brought Cloud. What if he forgets all about me?" Poppy brooded. She felt anchorless and unsettled knowing her pony would be so far away. He wouldn't be the first thing she saw every morning when she looked out of her bedroom window. She couldn't slip out of the back door after breakfast and give him her last triangle of toast. The days would seem empty and meaningless without the routine of mucking out, making up feeds, changing water and grooming. Most of all she would miss riding him. Poppy always felt as if she'd come home when she was on Cloud's back. They were a perfect fit.

She rested her forehead against the window and watched mile after endless mile speed by. It was early summer and the motorway verges were lush with new growth. Scarlett hadn't stopped talking since the minute they'd left and Poppy had tuned out long ago. She rolled up her fleece jacket into a makeshift pillow and had just drifted off to sleep when she was woken by the tinny American drawl of the McKeevers' sat nav.

"In one mile take the next right," it instructed.

Scarlett clutched Poppy's thigh. "We're nearly there,

Poppy! What's the place called again?"

"Oaklands Trekking Centre," Poppy said, batting her friend's hand away. She was suddenly plagued by worry. What if all the other riders were better than her? Scarlett had learnt to ride before she could walk, but Poppy had been riding for less than a year and was still inexperienced. What if everyone else was way older than them and too cool to make friends? But that wouldn't matter, she told herself. She still had Scarlett.

"What an idiot," Poppy's dad tutted, frowning into the rear-view mirror.

A silver saloon with its headlights flashing was a hair's breadth from their bumper.

"Why doesn't he overtake us if he's in that much of a hurry?" asked Poppy.

"Good question," said her dad. "Some people shouldn't be on the road."

He eased his foot off the accelerator and pulled over. As the other car passed they stared at the driver, a man in his fifties wearing dark glasses and leather gloves.

"Old enough to know better," Poppy's dad muttered.

"And he's on the phone!" shrieked Scarlett. Sure enough, a slim black mobile was tucked between his neck and shoulder.

The car accelerated hard past them with a throaty growl and kicked out a plume of black smoke from its exhaust. Poppy wrinkled her nose as her dad pulled back onto the road.

"In two hundred metres take the next right," the sat nav commanded.

Scarlett was on the edge of her seat. "Look, there's the turning!" she cried.

Poppy felt a flutter of nerves. She looked ahead and froze. Through the dazzling early summer sunshine she could see a blur of black and white. A large animal had bolted from their left and was heading at full pelt for the opposite side of the road.

"No!" Poppy screamed. The silver car was still accelerating, heading straight for the careering animal.

Scarlett's hand flew to her mouth. "He hasn't seen it. He's going to hit it!"

Just when a collision seemed inevitable there was a screech of brakes and the silver saloon slewed to a halt with centimetres to spare.

Poppy exhaled loudly. "That was close."

"What on earth was it?" said her dad.

"A cow, I think. I'll go and shoo it out of the way." Poppy unclipped her seatbelt and scrambled out, squinting into the sun. Before she'd taken more than a couple of steps up the road the silver car had roared off and the animal had disappeared. All that was left of the near disaster were some black skid marks on the tarmac and the smell of burning rubber.

Poppy was looking around in bewilderment when Scarlett joined her.

"Did you see which way it went?" she asked her friend.

Scarlett pointed at a blue and white sign, on which the words Oaklands Trekking Centre were painted in large letters. She looked up the long, potholed track behind them. "I think it went up there. But I'm not sure it was a cow, Poppy."

CHAPTER 2

"FRANK!" A woman's voice sliced through the warm air. "If you do that ONE MORE TIME there'll be trouble. And that's not a threat, it's a promise!"

Poppy and Scarlett paused at the five bar gate at the end of the driveway and looked at each other uncertainly. Poppy fumbled with the latch and as the gate swung open she saw a woman heading towards them, reading glasses on her forehead and a pencil stuck behind one ear. Following closely behind her was a black Shetland pony with a mischievous glint in his eye. The woman looked flustered but smiled as she held out her hand in greeting.

"You must be our competition winner. Poppy, isn't it? And Scarlett? I'm Nina Goddard, the owner of Oaklands. Nice to meet you."

As Poppy shook the woman's hand she noticed a red-brick chalet bungalow opposite an immaculately-

swept concrete yard, which was lined with two large
weather-boarded barns standing at right angles to
each other. Towering over the barns was a massive
oak tree, at least twenty metres tall and in full leaf.

Nina set off towards the bungalow, calling over her
shoulder, "Follow me, girls. Everyone else is already
here. We're just about to have lunch then I'll show
you your ponies for the week."

Poppy gave her dad a quick hug.

"See you both in a few days. Have fun," he told
them.

"Oh, we will," said Scarlett, still grinning. She
grabbed Poppy's arm and began dragging her after
Nina. "Come on, let's go and meet everyone."

Poppy's pulse quickened as Nina opened the door
to a large lounge and ushered them in. The buzz of
conversation petered out and she felt several pairs of
eyes swivel in her direction. Her palms felt sticky. She
wiped them on her jeans, hoping no-one would
notice. She knew she sometimes came across as
distant, even aloof. She usually relied on Scarlett to
chat enough for them both, but for once her best
friend was silent.

"Hi everyone. This is Scarlett and Poppy, our final
two trekkers. I'll let you say hello while I finish off in
the kitchen." Nina checked her watch. "Lunch will be
in about ten minutes."

Poppy gazed around the lounge, registering two
large squashy sofas, a scattering of beanbags in bright,

primary colours and a widescreen television fixed to the wall. And faces. Lots of faces.

She remembered the advice her stepmum Caroline had given her when she'd admitted she was worried about meeting the other trekkers.

"People love talking about themselves, Poppy. Ask them where they live, what their hobbies are and look like you're interested in their answers, even if you're not. Try not to hide behind your fringe. And remember to smile," she had advised. "It works every time, I promise."

Poppy licked her lips, pasted on a smile and took a step forward.

"Hello, I'm Poppy, and this is Scarlett. We've just driven up from Devon. What about you?" Her eyes swept around the room again, looking for a friendly face. Her gaze settled on a stunningly pretty girl, who was lounging on an orange beanbag. A couple of years older than Poppy and Scarlett, she was enviably tall and slim.

"I'm California. Cally for short." Cally gestured airily to the girl sitting next to her. "This is Chloe. And that's Jack and his little sister Jess." The others murmured hellos but Poppy was too overwhelmed to take in either their names or faces.

Cally flicked her long blonde fringe away from her face. She had clear, glowing skin, perfectly straight teeth and eyes that were neither blue nor grey but a blend of both. It was the kind of face that graced the covers of teen magazines. Poppy thought back to that morning, when she'd gazed critically at her own reflection in the bathroom mirror as she'd brushed her teeth. Sludge green eyes, pale skin that flushed at all the wrong moments, a heart-shaped face and shoulder-length brown hair that Poppy called mousey but Caroline assured her was caramel. Oh, and a globule of toothpaste on her chin. She rubbed the spot self-consciously and made herself speak.

"California. That's an unusual name."

Cally looked bored. Poppy realised she must get told this all the time and felt her cheeks redden.

"You could say. I've got my dippy mother to thank. It's because she's always wanted to go there. Fat chance."

Scarlett, still speechless, was looking at the older girl with something approaching awe. Poppy elbowed her in the ribs. She shook her head as if she was coming out of a trance.

"I think it's an amazing name. So unusual. I've never been to America. In fact I've never been anywhere. The only time we ever leave the farm is to visit all our ancient relatives, which is *so* boring. That's why I was so excited when Poppy won the riding holiday."

"You *won* the holiday?" said a stocky boy. He pointed the television remote control at her accusingly. "How?"

To her horror Poppy found she was the centre of attention again. "It was a short story competition," she said. "I've never won anything before. It was a complete surprise," she added, remembering to smile.

"Lucky you," drawled Cally. "I've spent the last six months working my backside off to pay for this holiday."

Poppy squirmed and examined her toes. She'd been over the moon when she'd arrived home from school a couple of months before and found a letter with a smudged London postmark propped against the fruit bowl. She'd ripped open the envelope and studied the single sheet of typewritten paper inside, her face wreathed in smiles. She'd read it so many times since that she knew it off by heart.

Dear Poppy,

Congratulations! I am delighted to inform you that your entry, Connemara Comes Home, has won first prize in Young Rider Magazine's short story competition. Your prize is a week-long riding holiday for two at Oaklands Trekking Centre in the Forest of Dean. Please contact our editorial assistant, Jane Gray, on the above number so we can make the necessary arrangements.

In the meantime, thank you for taking part in this year's competition.

Yours sincerely,
Marie Chidders, Editor-in-Chief

Poppy glanced at Cally and was dismayed to see the older girl looking her up and down with ill-disguised contempt. All the pride she'd felt at winning the competition trickled away, leaving her hollow. She

suddenly wished she'd spent the last six months
working her backside off to pay for the holiday, too.
It seemed much more real, more grown-up than
writing a silly story. Scarlett, completely oblivious to
Poppy's discomfort, pulled up a beanbag beside Cally
and sat down.

"I'd love to have a part-time job but Mum says I'm
not old enough. I've thought about getting a paper
round but I'd really like to work in a tea shop.
Imagine how many cakes you'd get to try. Where do
you work, Cally?"

Cally turned her attention to Scarlett. Shorter than
Poppy by half a head and sturdy where Poppy was
slight, Scarlett hated her freckles and auburn hair with
a passion. Poppy thought she was mad. Her hazel
eyes were the colour of a tiger's and her hair was the
russet red of beech trees in autumn. Poppy would
have chosen auburn over mousey any day.

Scarlett was as outgoing as Poppy was shy and her
non-stop chatter never failed to put people at their
ease. Poppy watched glumly as her best friend worked
her magic. Within minutes the sneering look had been
wiped from Cally's perfect face and she was smiling,
her voice warm as she described the riding school
where she worked all hours for paltry wages. Poppy
couldn't shake the feeling that Cally had put them
both through some kind of invisible test. A test that
Scarlett had obviously passed with flying colours and
Poppy had failed miserably.

She shuffled over to the nearest sofa and sat beside

a girl wearing a red polo shirt and navy jodhpurs. The girl smiled at her.

"Have you brought your story with you? I'd love to read it," she said.

As Poppy nodded she caught a whiff of honeysuckle from the open window. She was transported home to Riverdale, where the climber's greeny-grey leaves and light yellow flowers, tinged with the barest hint of pink, trailed over a trellis archway that led to Caroline's vegetable garden. She pictured her stepmother carefully weeding between rows of tiny lettuce and pea plants, her blonde hair scraped off her face in an untidy updo, her brow furrowed in concentration. Charlie would probably be sat astride the old stone wall that protected the vegetable garden from the worst of the westerly winds, pretending he was a cowboy. Her dad would be sitting on the old wooden bench that had been turned silver by the sun, reading the Sunday papers. She saw Cloud and Chester in her mind's eye, grazing side by side in their paddock to the side of the house. Watching over them all was the Riverdale tor, dominating the huge Dartmoor skyline. Poppy knew the tor so well she could have marched straight to the cairn at the top blindfolded.

She looked over at her best friend, seeking reassurance. But Scarlett's head was bent towards Cally, her voice suffused with laughter as she regaled the older girl with stories of her pony Blaze. Poppy felt a snag of homesickness, as sharp as barbed wire, pierce her insides.

CHAPTER 3

Poppy had no appetite by the time she took a seat next to Scarlett at the long pine table in Nina's scruffy kitchen. Sitting at the head of the table was a girl with the face of a cherub, who was noisily demolishing a plate of sausages and baked beans. Most of the sauce was smeared around her rosy cheeks. She smiled, pointed her fork at the older children as they piled in and shouted, "Mum! New people!"

"This is my daughter Lydia. She's four," said Nina.

"Nearly five," grumbled Lydia through a mouthful of beans.

Nina plucked a wet wipe from a packet on the kitchen worktop and wiped it across Lydia's outraged face before she had time to duck. The resulting howls of protest made the girl in the red polo shirt giggle nervously.

"Take a seat everyone. Your mum said you're a

vegan, Cally. I've cooked your vegetarian sausages in a separate pan."

Cally looked even more incensed than Lydia. "Mum may be a vegan. She is also an old hippy. I, on the other hand, am neither. I'll have the same sausages as everyone else, please."

Nina passed around plates of sausages, beans and chips. Poppy pushed the food around her plate and tried not to think about home. Instead she took the opportunity to scrutinize their fellow pony trekkers.

Sitting directly opposite and tucking into his lunch with gusto was the stocky boy. He looked about twelve or thirteen. Poppy fished around in her memory for his name. James or Josh? No, Jack. That was it. He had a bullish, square jaw and thick black eyebrows that almost met in the middle. From the snippets of conversation Poppy could catch he was telling the girl to his left about his current fantasy football team. Sitting opposite Scarlett was the girl in the red polo shirt. She must be Jack's younger sister. She had the same determined chin. Jess, Poppy remembered. She guessed she was probably about ten.

The girl to Jack's left was stifling a yawn as he blathered on about penalty shoot outs and goal differentials. She was about the same age as Jess and was small and slight with direct brown eyes. She caught Poppy watching her and grimaced theatrically. Poppy suppressed a smile and turned to Scarlett, but her best friend was still talking to Cally. All Poppy could see was the back of her head.

Nina banged the table with her fork, halting the wave of chat. "I'd like to take this opportunity to welcome you to Oaklands. I hope you will all fall in love with the place as deeply as I did. I can still remember how excited I was when I saw photos of the house and yard in an estate agents' window two years ago. I grew up in the Forest of Dean and always wanted to move back. I loved the fact that the house was miles from its nearest neighbours yet the forest was right on the doorstep.

"I thought the place was beyond our means but I must have caught my bank manager on a good day." Nina gave the ghost of a smile. "We started running our trekking holidays last summer and we're now in our second season. We love it here, don't we, Lyd?" Lydia nodded vigorously. Poppy was surprised to see Nina's eyes cloudy with tears. She wondered if anyone else had noticed, but they were all still ploughing their way through their lunch. Nina tucked a kiss-curl behind Lydia's ear and continued.

"The Forest of Dean is fantastic for hacking. We often see deer in the forest and if we're really lucky we might see a wild boar."

"A wild boar?" repeated Jess, her eyes wide. "Aren't they dangerous?"

"Well, yes, they can be, especially if they have young to protect. But they are very secretive and largely nocturnal so the chances of coming across one are pretty slim," Nina assured her.

"But what if we do? Won't they charge at the ponies?" Jess persisted.

"Who cares if they do," said her brother scornfully. "We could out-gallop them, no problem."

"They're faster than you think," said Nina. "The trick is not to antagonise them in the first place. They usually hide in the undergrowth, so if we stick to the paths we'll be fine." She noticed the lines creasing the girl's brow. "Don't worry, Jess. I ride in the forest every day and I've only seen wild boar twice, and that was from a distance. We'll be fine."

Nina smiled at them all. "I've got some lovely routes planned for the week. We'll set off straight after breakfast each morning and we'll cover about twelve miles each day, stopping halfway for a picnic lunch. All the horses have saddle bags and I'll pack your lunches in them." She pointed to an untidy heap of leather saddle bags next to a pile of unopened brown envelopes on the kitchen worktop. "We'll be back at about four each afternoon and once you've finished your yard duties your time is your own."

The girl next to Jack stuck her hand in the air.

"Yes, Chloe?" Nina asked.

"How many horses do you have?"

"Eight. My thoroughbred, McFly, Lydia's Shetland, Frank, and our six trekking ponies. I'll show you your ponies after lunch and we'll go for a gentle hack this afternoon so you can get a feel for them."

"Will we be having a canter today?" Jack asked.

"We'll see how we go. You've all done quite a bit of

riding, which is great. The group I had last week was a nightmare. One girl had never sat on a horse before. At least if you're all about the same level we can have some decent rides."

There was a jangle of cutlery on plates. Nina stood up. "All finished? Leave your plates and glasses on the draining board and I'll give you a tour of the house and stables."

There were four small bedrooms, each with bunk beds, at the back of the house. Poppy and Scarlett's room looked out over the yard.

"Leave the unpacking, Poppy. We'll do it later," Scarlett said impatiently as they changed into their jodhpurs. "Let's go and meet the ponies."

They caught up with the others outside the first of the two bitumen-black barns. It had been divided into loose boxes, three each down the two long sides and one at either end. Nina stopped at the first box. A bay horse appeared over the door and nibbled her hair. "This is McFly. He's ten. I bought him as a yearling and produced him myself. We used to event but we don't get the opportunity to compete these days."

McFly towered above them. "How big is he?" wondered Scarlett.

"He's 17.2. Frank can actually walk under him. But he's a gentle giant. Just costs me a fortune in hay and feed. And his rugs are the size of small marquees. Now this is Blue. She's your ride for the week, Cally. She is sharp but I remember when you booked you said you were an experienced rider so she shouldn't be anything you can't handle. I think you'll have a lot of fun on her."

Poppy stood on tiptoes to peer over Cally's shoulder. Standing in the corner of her box, delicately nibbling on some hay, was a rose grey Arab mare, whose dished head, silky mane and tail and wide-spaced, intelligent eyes exuded elegance.

Cally was delighted. Scarlett looked impressed. Poppy felt a twinge of envy.

"Chloe, you're next." Chloe looked as if she was about to burst with excitement as Nina showed her a chestnut gelding called Rusty who had a white star in the centre of his forehead and two white socks. "He's a real schoolmaster, as honest as they come," Nina said.

Chloe's eyes were dancing. "He's beautiful," she breathed.

Jack's sister, Jess, was given Willow, a dun mare with soot black points. She was a Welsh Section B who was great for trekking and never put a foot wrong, Nina told her.

Jack's pony was a sturdy liver chestnut lightweight cob called Rocky. "Cool," he said, nodding his approval. They left him in Rocky's box as they crossed the barn to the last two loose boxes. Poppy could sense Scarlett's excitement. "Scarlett, you'll be riding Topaz. She's a New Forest cross." Poppy and Scarlett looked over the door and saw a pretty palomino mare with her head buried in a hayrack.

Scarlett's freckled face split into a grin. "Oo, I've always wanted a palomino!"

"Topaz is the name of a golden gemstone. It suits her, don't you think? I'm glad you like her," said Nina.

Poppy felt a frisson of anticipation as she followed Nina to the end of the barn. She'd been impressed by all the trekking ponies. Nina obviously had an eye for real quality. And as the competition winner, surely she'd be given the best of the lot? She crossed her fingers, wishing for a flashy Arab like Blue, preferably jet black, although she wasn't fussy, any colour would do.

A metal anti-weaving grill was attached to the door of the last loose box.

"Here's Beau," Nina announced with a flourish, "He's all yours, Poppy."

Poppy stepped forward. She realised she was holding her breath. She held onto two of the metal bars and peered through them. A jolt of shock hit her in the stomach with the velocity of a high speed train. Nina had to be kidding, right?

"Very funny," she said. "So where is he really?"

Nina looked puzzled. "That's him. That's Beau."

Poppy looked into the loose box again and back at Nina's face. No telltale smirk or giveaway crinkling of the eyes. She was deadly serious.

Realising Nina was waiting for her reaction she forced a smile and said in a strangulated voice, "Hello Beau."

At the sound of his name a piebald cob with a long,

tangled mane and a wall eye stuck his head over the loose box door. He yawned, flashing a set of yellowing teeth.

A feeling of bitter disappointment crept from Poppy's head to her toes, along with the uncanny suspicion that she had seen this horse before, although for the life of her she couldn't think where.

Then she remembered the silver saloon car's squealing brakes and her heart sank even further. Poppy looked desperately at Scarlett, and was disconcerted to see her best friend's mouth twitching, as if she was biting back a bubble of laughter.

And finally Scarlett confirmed her worst fears. "Hey Poppy, I think we may have found the amazing disappearing cow."

CHAPTER 4

"Someone was having a laugh when they called him Beau," said Cally drily, looking over from Blue's loose box. "He's no oil painting, is he?"

"Beauty is as beauty does," said Nina tartly. "Don't be too quick to judge him." She smiled at Poppy. "Beau is one in a million. He may not be the prettiest horse on the yard but he has the heart of a lion and if he decides he likes you he'll do absolutely anything for you."

An image of Cloud's handsome grey head swam in front of Poppy's eyes. She'd only been gone a matter of hours but it felt like she hadn't seen him for months. She looked again at the piebald cob. His large head was black with a wide white blaze running down his face. His forehead was flat and broad. The eye that wasn't blue was as dark as mahogany. Under his long, straggly mane Poppy could see a crested neck set in a deep, broad chest. All four legs were white from the knee down and he had thick, muddy feathers. Other than his pink nose and his blue wall eye he was completely monochrome. Poppy held out a hand for him to sniff but he ignored her and turned back to his hay.

"The only one you haven't met is Frank. He must be around here somewhere." Nina stepped into the yard, put two fingers in her mouth and whistled. The black Shetland pony Poppy and Scarlett had seen earlier appeared from the open door of the second barn, covered in hay. "Frank! Not again! I can't afford for you to be helping yourself to hay whenever you feel like it! Come here, you monster." The pony waddled over to Nina and she scratched his poll. "This is Frank. What he lacks in height he makes up for in mischief. His speciality is untying knots and unbolting doors so you all need to keep an extra eye on him. He and Beau came together as a job lot at auction. They're inseparable." As she spoke the Shetland bustled over to Beau's door. The piebald whickered and started eating the hay stuck in Frank's bushy mane. Everyone except Poppy laughed. She seemed to have lost her sense of humour.

"Right, let's get tacked up," Nina said. "Lydia's coming with us today but during the week she'll be with her childminder so we'll be able to up the pace."

Poppy followed Scarlett into the tack room. Her friend took one look at her miserable face and frowned.

"What's wrong, Poppy?"

"What's wrong? What do you think's wrong? Nina must be out of her mind to think that old clodhopper is any good as a trekking pony. He should be pulling a cart! No wonder I thought he was a cow."

"He looks sweet." As Scarlett reached for Topaz's bridle Poppy saw a flash of annoyance cross her face. It cleared so quickly she wondered if she'd imagined it.

"You might find he's a lovely ride," Scarlett said, her tone placatory. "At least give him a chance."

"And do I have a choice?" she growled.

She balanced Beau's saddle on her hip, swung his bridle over her shoulder and, with some trepidation, walked over to the cob's loose box. He had finished the hay in Frank's mane and had turned back to his hayrack. She patted his neck hesitantly and he gave her a baleful stare. It was as if his blue wall eye could see straight through her with X-ray vision - and was singularly unimpressed by what he saw. He took a step sideways and stood on her left foot, sending bolts of pain shooting up her calf.

"Ow!" she cried, leaning on his shoulder to make him move. But it was like pushing a brick wall. He wasn't going anywhere. "Please move, Beau!" she gasped, her foot still pinned to the ground by an iron-clad hoof the size of a dinner plate. Beau ignored her and began chomping on his hay. Poppy looked around her helplessly. At this rate she'd be here all day, her foot being squashed thinner and thinner until it was as flat as filo pastry. She tried again but Beau didn't move. Outside the barn she could hear the others' chatter as they tacked up and mounted. Feeling increasingly desperate she remembered the Polos in her pocket and waved the packet under Beau's nose. He immediately lifted his foot off her jodhpur boot, gave her a hefty nudge and nearly bit her little finger off in his haste to snaffle the mint she offered him.

Nina's face appeared over the loose box door. She frowned when she saw that Beau still wasn't tacked up. "Do you need a hand?"

Poppy felt her cheeks flush. "No, thanks. I won't be a minute."

Nina disappeared and Poppy eyed the cob with dislike. "I don't want any more nonsense," she told him firmly. "And if you're good you can have another Polo. Alright?"

If horses could have shrugged with indifference Poppy would have bet money that's what Beau was doing right now. But at least he stood still as she whizzed around him, putting on his saddle and bridle, tightening his girth and pulling down his stirrup leathers. Soon she was leading him out of his box into the yard, where everyone else was standing waiting for her.

"Good, you're ready. The mounting block is over there," said Nina, pointing to the opposite side of the yard. Poppy felt everyone's eyes on her as she led Beau over, checked the girth again and pulled herself gingerly into the saddle. At fifteen hands, Beau was slightly taller than Cloud, and felt enormous compared to her fine-boned Connemara. Poppy cringed with embarrassment when Lydia shouted, "She's finally ready! Can we go now?"

"OK everyone. Just a few house rules," said Nina. "I'll ride up front with Frank and Lydia on a leading rein, then Topaz and Blue, Willow and Rusty and finally Rocky and Beau bringing up the rear. We'll be riding along country lanes for a mile or so before we reach the forest so please be polite to drivers, and once we're on the bridleways keep to the tracks and stay in line. Right, follow me."

Nina turned McFly out of the yard. Poppy gathered up her reins and squeezed with her heels but Beau stood stubbornly still as the others filed in behind the bay thoroughbred and began walking down the track to the road. When Rocky's liver chestnut rump had disappeared through the gates and Beau was still refusing to budge Poppy kicked as hard as she could. The cob grunted and set off at a snail's pace behind him.

Beau's rolling gait was nothing like Cloud's graceful stride. Poppy wondered if this was what camels felt like to ride. Rocky was already twenty metres ahead and Poppy kicked again. Beau reluctantly broke into a trot and Poppy bumped up and down for a few strides until she found a rhythm and started to rise. She could feel a sheen of sweat across her forehead and her hands were clammy. Up ahead Scarlett was riding alongside Cally, who sat gracefully astride the elegant Blue. Scarlett's face was animated and she paused every now and again to run her hand along Topaz's golden neck. She was clearly having the time of her life. Poppy looked down gloomily at Beau's tangled mane and feathered feet. Why didn't Nina give her an old carthorse and be done with it, she fumed.

Some holiday this was turning out to be.

The others had disappeared into one of the wide forest tracks that fed into the road like tributaries into a river when Poppy heard a car behind her. She heaved Beau to a halt and waited for the car to pass. Beau took the opportunity to grab a mouthful of cow parsley and she was leaning forward so she could pull it out of his mouth when she became aware of a silver bonnet drawing alongside them. Straightening her back she stared at the man who had almost ploughed into Beau just a few hours before. But he obviously hadn't made the connection, and to her surprise opened his electric window.

"Excuse me, I seem to be lost. I'm looking for Oaklands."

Poppy fixed her eyes on Beau's ears and said nothing.

"Oaklands," he repeated. "Nina Goddard's place. According to the map it's down here somewhere. Do you know where it is?"

Poppy could see a map, a clipboard and the man's

mobile phone on the passenger seat beside him. Oaklands was in all likelihood on the map anyway, she supposed.

"It's about a mile back that way," she said finally, pointing behind her.

"Are you her daughter? Lydia, isn't it?"

Poppy shook her head.

"Do you happen to know if Mrs Goddard is in?"

"She won't be back for at least a couple of hours." Beau stuck his head through the window and sneezed, spraying the man's shiny suit with droplets of snot. Poppy pulled his head back hastily.

"Beau! Sorry about that. Can I give her a message?"

Wiping his trousers fastidiously, the man looked up in irritation. "What? No, don't bother. I'll track her down soon enough." The window slid shut and the car pulled away. Poppy shrugged, kicked Beau on and they trotted down the lane. Nina and McFly met them as they crossed the road and joined the forest track.

"There you are!" said Nina. "I thought I'd better come and find you. Everything OK?"

"There was a man looking for you," said Poppy.

Nina's forehead creased. "A man?"

"Yes, in a silver car. I saw him earlier as well. He overtook us on the way here and almost caused an accident." Poppy wasn't sure if Nina knew Beau had been out on the road and felt it best not to worry her.

"What did he say?" Nina asked.

"He asked for directions so I told him where you lived. But when I asked him if he wanted me to give

32

you a message he said no, he'd track you down himself."

The colour sapped from Nina's face. "Track me down?"

"Yes, that's what he said. He asked me if I was Lydia."

"He knew Lydia's name?" she asked faintly.

"He didn't seem very friendly, actually." Poppy considered the encounter. "Did I do the right thing?"

"I should have known it was only a matter of time," Nina said, half to herself. She looked at Poppy, her eyes anxious. "Please don't mention this to anyone. With any luck we'll make it to the end of the week." McFly pawed the ground impatiently and Nina gathered her reins. "Come on, we'd better get back to the others."

CHAPTER 5

Poppy didn't have a chance to wonder what the man wanted and why Nina had seemed so troubled. All her energies were concentrated on keeping up with the rest of the riders. Never before had she had to work so hard in the saddle. Even Flynn, the stout Dartmoor pony she'd learnt to ride on, was more bouncy than Beau. No matter how much she kicked his piebald sides the cob refused to alter his pace from the leisurely rolling walk that she swore was making her seasick.

As they ambled along a grassy forest track that cut a swathe through lofty pine trees Beau snatched at his bit and stretched his neck down. Assuming he had an itch, Poppy let the reins slide through her fingers. But the cob had other things on his mind, and began snatching up mouthfuls of grass. "Oh no, you don't," she told him, hauling at his reins. But he ignored her and carried on grazing. It took Nina to re-appear alongside them and reach over to grab his right rein before he lifted his head.

"You need to be firmer with him, Poppy," Nina said. "I'm afraid he does try it on with new riders. You have to earn his respect." She looked at her watch. "Goodness, look at the time! We really need to get going. Do you think you can try to keep up?"

"I'll do my best," Poppy said through gritted teeth. "Although if you'd given me a half-decent horse to ride it wouldn't be an issue," she muttered as Nina took Frank's lead rein from Cally and re-joined the front of the group.

Poppy spent the rest of the ride lagging behind the others, like a dawdling toddler trailing behind her parents. Only when they turned back down the grassy track towards home did Beau seem to wake up, and when the others broke into a canter he grabbed the bit and set off behind them like a racehorse out of its stall when the starter's pistol was fired. Poppy, thrown back in the saddle by the force of his acceleration, clutched the reins and a handful of his long mane for good measure as he thundered along the track, his feathers flying. The breeze felt cool on her pink cheeks and she began to relax into his long, loping gait. He must be the closest thing on earth to a rocking horse, she thought, as they gained ground on Rocky and Jack.

Poppy stood up in her stirrups as Beau's stride lengthened and the beginnings of a smile crept across her face. She realised with surprise that she was actually enjoying herself. But her pleasure was short-lived. The cob spooked at a clump of oxeye daisies growing in the long grass to the side of the track, slamming on his brakes and dropping his shoulder like an actor taking a bow. Poppy, her weight already forward, was thrown out of the saddle and landed heavily on a clump of thistles. Still holding Beau's reins, she heaved herself upright. He watched innocently as she plucked a couple of thorny spikes from her backside. She shot him a filthy look and gathered her reins, hoping she could jump back on before anyone noticed. But it was too late. Jack had slowed Rocky to a walk and was calling to Nina. Poppy just caught his words as they were carried away by the wind.

"It's Poppy again. She's fallen off this time."

The sun was low in the sky by the time they began evening stables. As Poppy mucked out Beau's loosebox, scrubbed out and re-filled his water bucket and re-stocked his hayrack she thought about the man in the silver saloon car. He'd looked harmless enough so why had Nina been so worried when she'd found out he was looking for her? She'd seemed particularly upset when Poppy had told her he'd mistaken her for Lydia. And what did she mean about making it to the end of the week?

Poppy was dying to tell Scarlett about the mystery man and seized her chance when they changed for dinner.

"He seemed a bit...strange," said Poppy. Scarlett was facing the small mirror over the chest of drawers, her back to Poppy. "Hey, wait a minute. Since when did you start wearing make-up?"

Scarlett eyed her in the mirror. "Cally lent me some. I thought I'd give it a try. Is that a problem?"

"No, of course not. I was only asking. Don't be so defensive. Anyway, he looked really angry when Beau sneezed all over his shiny suit."

"I'm not surprised. Wouldn't you be?"

"But what do you think he wanted? And why did Nina look so worried?" Poppy said. But she could tell that Scarlett wasn't really listening. She was too busy striking poses in front of the mirror, her newly pearlescent lips catching the light as she pouted like a catwalk model. Finally satisfied with her appearance, she turned to face Poppy and gave a little twirl.

"How do I look?"

Poppy considered her best friend. Scarlett had swept pale pink blusher over her cheekbones and had smudged black eyeliner along her eye-lids before applying several layers of mascara. The smoky look accentuated her hazel eyes. She looked much older than her twelve years. Poppy wasn't sure she liked it. Scarlett tousled her hair, letting her fringe fall over one eye.

"Well?" she demanded, her hands on her hips.

"It's OK I suppose, but I prefer the natural look. Come on, we're going to be late for our tea."

The topic of conversation over the dinner table revolved around the Oaklands horses. Everyone else was delighted with their rides, which made Poppy feel doubly short-changed to have been given Beau. That night, as they lay in their bunk beds, Poppy railed against Nina for giving her the ungainly cob.

"Honestly Scarlett, it's like riding a socking great elephant," she moaned. "He's about as responsive as a dodo."

But if she was hoping to elicit any sympathy from her best friend she was out of luck.

"Did you know Cally went to a John Whittaker showjumping clinic last year? It was a fourteenth birthday present from her granny, lucky thing."

"Really?" said Poppy. "But I mean, Scarlett, you're alright. Topaz is great. Beau is an absolute nightmare. Do you think Nina would swap him for one of the other horses if I asked? After all, I did win the short story competition."

"Cally says I've got a really nice seat, much better than the girls my age who go to her riding school," Scarlett continued.

"Her riding school now, is it? I thought she just mucked out in return for the occasional ride," said Poppy grumpily.

"She's got a proper job as a groom and she's going to train to be an instructor. I think she'd be really good, don't you?"

"Scarlett! Do you think Nina would give me

another horse if I complained about Beau?"

Scarlett finally turned her attention to her friend. "Nina has a soft spot for him, that's what Cally reckons anyway. I think you should give him another chance."

Poppy stuck her tongue out at the dark shadow of Scarlett's mattress above her and pulled her duvet over her head. "Why not give me Blue and let the wonderful California have Beau? See how she gets on with the great clodhopper," she grumbled into her pillow.

Scarlett, who was having the time of her life, either didn't hear or chose not to answer. She turned over and promptly fell asleep while Poppy seethed quietly in the bunk bed below.

CHAPTER 6

The early morning dew had turned cobwebs on the grass into glistening panels of lace that reminded Poppy of the delicate antimacassars on the two floral-patterned armchairs in her old friend Tory's small flat. Her jodhpur boots were quickly soaked through as she marched across the paddock Beau shared with Frank and Rocky, Beau's cob-sized headcollar on her shoulder and a Polo going sticky in her right palm. The piebald was tearing up tussocks of the dewy grass as if he'd been without food for a week. Poppy clicked her tongue and opened her hand.

"Look, I've brought you a Polo," she told him. "And if you behave yourself I've plenty more where they came from. But I don't want any more bad behaviour."

Poppy had woken in a peevish mood. Her body felt as though it'd been pulled on a rack, her left foot was a livid shade of purple and she swore she still had a thorn in her right buttock. Added to that, Scarlett's incessant chirpiness was starting to wear thin and she wasn't relishing the prospect of another day spent doing battle with the ill-mannered cob.

Beau lifted his shaggy head and Poppy slipped the headcollar over his muzzle, buckled up the strap and gave him the mint. "Try not to bite my hand off this time." Beau whickered. "Was that for me?" she asked him in surprise. But he was looking over her shoulder at Frank, who had appeared from the other side of the field. "Of course it wasn't. You like me about as much as I like you. Come on, I don't want to be the last one ready today."

Topaz and Blue had been tied up next to each other. Poppy tugged on Beau's leadrope and he followed her unenthusiastically to the other side of the yard, depositing a large dropping on the concrete the minute she'd finished tying a quick release knot. She cleared it up before scooting over to the tack room in search of some grooming kit and spent the next fifteen minutes trying to brush the mud from Beau's thick coat. Frank was wandering around the yard stealing brushes and hoofpicks to the amusement of the others, who had already started tacking up.

Poppy mouth was gritty with dust and she had a horrible feeling that she was covered in a fine film of the mud she'd just brushed from Beau. Sighing loudly, she walked over to fetch his tack, stopping to listen to

Scarlett and Cally on her way. The older girl was telling Scarlett about the riding school where she worked.

"The horses I ride are all thoroughbreds that used to race on the flat. Rose - she's the owner - buys up ex-racehorses and I help her re-train them before she sells them on."

"Really? Ex-racehorses? That's amazing."

Cally acknowledged Scarlett's admiration with a careless dip of her head. She had the kind of easy confidence that Poppy found incredibly intimidating and usually left her tongue-tied. But she remembered her stepmum Caroline's advice, edged over and said, "Scarlett says you want to train as a riding instructor when you leave school, Cally."

The older girl gave her a lofty look and nodded. "Yes, but my ultimate ambition is to be picked for the British showjumping team."

"Wow, that's impressive. Do you do much jumping now?"

"I started affiliated classes this spring. The trouble with training the ex-racers is that the minute they're jumping well Rose sells them and I have to start all over again. I need to find a way of getting my own horse, but Mum's always broke and I don't even earn a fraction of the minimum wage at the stables."

Scarlett had disappeared into the tack room. Poppy tried to look sympathetic. "These things have a habit of working out. That's what my stepmum always says, anyway."

"Easy for you to say. Scarlett told me your dad works for the BBC and is always on the television. You must be rolling in it," Cally said bitterly. She untied Blue, pulled her stirrup leathers down roughly and sprang into the saddle, shooting Poppy a scathing look as she did.

Poppy coloured and disappeared into the tack room in search of Scarlett, who was humming to herself as she pulled on her hat.

"I wish you hadn't told Cally what my dad did. She's just accused me of being loaded. Chance would be a fine thing," she grumbled.

"You are, compared with Cally," said Scarlett bluntly. "Her dad left when she was a baby. Her mum is a part-time carer and they live in a council flat. Cally says they don't have two pennies to rub together."

"Well, it's no reason for her to have a go at me. It's not my fault her mum can't get a decent job."

"Poppy! That's a terrible thing to say. You know nothing about Cally or her mum. Sometimes you should try thinking before you speak." Scarlett brushed past Poppy as she stomped out of the tack room. Poppy felt a stab of hurt and went to follow her friend, but was deterred by the set of Scarlett's shoulders. Instead she sat on a feed bin and watched a pair of swallows swooping in and out of their mud nest high on one of the rafters. Hearing the clatter of hooves she heaved Beau's saddle from its rack, picked up his bridle and headed back out into the yard. The sun was bright after the gloom of the tack room and she paused for a moment to rub her eyes.

Nina stepped in front of her, obscuring the sun. "Where's Beau, Poppy?"

"He's over -" she began, but the words dried up as she looked across the yard in dismay. The loop of string she'd tied Beau to was flapping gently in the wind and the piebald cob was nowhere to be seen.

Poppy looked around her wildly. "I left him tied up outside the barn while I popped in to get his tack. He must be here somewhere." She became aware that the others had stopped what they were doing to listen.

"Are you sure you tied him up properly?" Nina said, running her hand through her hair.

"Yes!" cried Poppy, already doubting herself. She felt everyone's eyes on her and thought longingly of Riverdale, where it was just her, Cloud and Chester and no-one questioned her every move.

"He can't have gone far. The gate to the track's closed," Chloe pointed out.

"Wait a minute - Frank's gone, too!" said Jess.

"I might have known," said Nina grimly. "Follow me," she told Poppy, heading for the hay barn. She threw open the double doors to reveal Frank and Beau, who were happily working their way through a bale of hay.

"I did warn you that Frank was a little Houdini," Nina said. "Next time pass the end of the leadrope through the loop of the quick release knot. Frank can still undo that if he's got long enough to figure it out, but at least it buys you some extra time." She smiled briefly at Poppy, who was willing the earth to swallow her up. "It's OK, no harm done, and you'll know for next time. She glanced at her watch. "Come on everyone, let's see if we can be ready in five minutes."

Soon they were clip-clopping down the lane. Or, if Poppy was being accurate, the others were clip-clopping down the lane and Beau was trundling along in his own little world, helping himself to mouthfuls of cow parsley and taking no notice of his rider and her efforts to chivvy him up. She doubted the cob even remembered she was still on board. She was so used to seeing Cloud's small grey pricked ears in front of her that she kept doing a double take when she saw Beau's enormous black ears flicking back and forth. Cloud's silver mane was neatly pulled and lay smoothly to his off-side. Despite her best efforts to tame it, Beau's thick mane was flopping over on both sides and was already starting to tangle. Poppy had spent the last few weeks counting the days until the riding holiday. Now she was counting the hours until she returned home. She gathered up the reins and attempted to kick Beau into a trot.

"Come on, you lazy toad," she said, clicking her tongue. Beau gave a shake of his large head and broke into an unenthusiastic jog. She caught up with Scarlet and Cally, who were riding two abreast down the quiet country lane. Blue flicked her grey tail in displeasure and snaked her head at Beau, her ears back and her teeth bared.

"Oh, Nina says Blue doesn't like Beau," said Cally.

"It might be better if you don't ride next to us."

"Oh, right," Poppy said, flustered.

"Come and ride next to me and Chloe," said Jess. "Willow and Rusty won't mind."

Grateful not to be lagging behind on her own yet again Poppy manoeuvred Beau alongside the two girls.

"Do you have your own pony at home, Poppy?" asked Chloe.

"Yes, I have a dappled grey Connemara called Cloud. And a donkey called Chester. What about you two?"

Chloe shook her head. "I wish I did. I have riding lessons every Saturday, and I know I'm lucky to have that, but it's not the same, is it?"

Poppy smiled sympathetically. "No, it's not. I know exactly how you feel. When we lived in London all I ever wanted was my own pony. I didn't even have riding lessons until we moved to Devon."

"That's why my mum and dad gave me the riding holiday for my tenth birthday. They said it would be cheaper than buying me my own pony. I've been looking forward to it for *months*," said Chloe, hugging Rusty's neck.

"What about you, Jess?" Poppy asked. She was pretty sure the answer was yes. Although Chloe sat in the correct riding position and kept her back straight, her heels down and her hands steady, her body was rigid and her grip on Rusty's reins was tight. It betrayed the fact that she was a novice, only used to riding once a week. Jess, on the other hand, had the relaxed, easy seat of someone who'd been riding all her life. She had Willow on a long rein and her body moved in rhythm with the dun mare's swinging walk.

"Jack and I share our sister Lucy's old pony, Magic," said Jess, confirming Poppy's hunch. "Lucy's at university and hardly rides these days. Jack's only really interested in bombing around at our pony club with his friends, so I get to ride Magic most. He's a bit old and creaky, but I love him."

Poppy smiled and began to relax. As they wound their way along forest tracks behind the others she found herself telling the girls about Cloud.

"Last summer we moved from London to a cottage on the edge of Dartmoor. It's next to Scarlett's farm," she added, glancing ahead to her friend, who was still deep in conversation with Cally. Poppy's smile faded and she turned back to the two girls.

"The cottage is called Riverdale and it used to belong to an old lady called Tory Wickens, who bought Cloud for her grand-daughter Caitlyn. But Caitlyn was killed when they fell during a hunter trial."

"Killed!" said Chloe, aghast. "What happened?"

Poppy remembered the rainy day the previous autumn when Tory, her weathered old face streaked with tears, had described the events of that terrible day. Caitlyn, a talented young rider with masses of potential, had been flying around the course on her beloved Connemara when he had lost his footing in the mud as the pair jumped a drop fence.

"He somersaulted over, throwing Caitlyn underneath him. Tory said she died instantly."

"That's awful!" said Jess, her eyes wide.

"How old was she?" asked Chloe.

"Thirteen. A year older than me and Scarlett."

The two girls fell silent. Poppy knew they would be imagining the sirens, the ambulance lurching over the uneven, muddy course, the screens being erected around the young rider as the paramedics shielded her lifeless body from the spectators. Poppy knew, because she had imagined the scene countless times herself.

"Poor Caitlyn," whispered Jess.

"I know. Tory never really got over it."

"What happened to Cloud?" asked Chloe.

"He was bought by a local famer, a man called George Blackstone. He's as nasty as they come. People say he beats the ponies he buys and sells and I can quite believe it.

"Cloud managed to escape from the Blackstone farm and spent the next few years living wild on Dartmoor. I saw him from a distance the day we moved to Riverdale and spent weeks trying to catch him. In the end he was rounded up with the Dartmoor ponies and Blackstone sold him at auction, but my dad was there and bought him for me."

"Wow, it's like a fairy-tale. Why do things like that never happen to me?" said Chloe wistfully.

"Ah, but it wasn't quite as simple as it sounds. He'd broken a bone in his foot so there was a chance I might never be able to ride him. He had to have months of box rest. And then last Christmas, while I was in bed with the flu, my brother Charlie accidentally fed him unsoaked sugerbeet and he was so ill with colic that I thought he was going to die."

After being virtually ignored and then admonished by Scarlett, Poppy was gratified by the rapt expressions on the two girls' faces. "We were completely snowed in so the vet couldn't get to us," she told them.

"What did you do?" Chloe asked, open-mouthed.

"I kept walking him every half an hour. I'd remembered reading that was what you're supposed to do. Luckily it did the trick and the colic passed. His fracture healed earlier this year and I finally started riding him this spring."

"You saved his life," breathed Jess.

"Yes, I suppose I did," Poppy replied. She sat taller in the saddle and smiled modestly at Chloe and Jess. Unfortunately Beau chose that precise moment to sidestep into the trees to avoid a puddle and Poppy was almost knocked out of the saddle by the low-hanging bough of a sweet chestnut tree. She cursed under her breath as the whippy branch struck her cheek painfully.

"Are you alright?" Chloe asked in concern.

"Yes, I'm fine," she answered, rubbing her cheek. Beau swung back onto the path, completely unaware that he'd almost knocked her flying.

Or did he know exactly what he'd done? Poppy

couldn't be sure. All she knew for certain was that she missed Cloud with all her heart and would have given anything to have swapped the bumbling Beau for her beautiful Connemara.

CHAPTER 7

Poppy's cheek was still smarting as she untacked Beau and brushed him down after their ride.

"What happened to you? It looks like you've been slapped in the face by a wet fish," smirked Cally as she walked past the cob on her way to the tack room. Jack, who was untacking Rocky nearby, sniggered.

"No, Beau just chose to go the scenic route through the trees. But I'm glad you both find it so amusing," Poppy muttered, bending down to pick up one of Beau's feet so they couldn't see her face. Beau turned his head and nipped her backside.

"Ow! What did you do that for?" she cried, dropping both his foot and the hoofpick, which skittered onto the concrete. She heard Cally stifling a snort of laughter as she crossed the yard to Blue. Poppy glared at her retreating back and then looked daggers at Beau, who was nibbling his leadrope unperturbed.

"You could show me some loyalty. As if I haven't got enough to put up with," she told him, tugging at the quick release knot and dragging him towards the field gate. Nina joined them as they passed the hay barn. She gave Beau's ear an affectionate rub and smiled at Poppy.

"How are you finding Beau?"

Poppy scratched around for something positive to say and failed. "He's certainly like nothing I've ever ridden before."

"Good, I'm so glad you like him." They passed under the old oak. "Have I told you about our oak trees here in the Forest of Dean?"

Poppy was glad to have something to take her mind off Cally, Scarlett and Beau, and shook her head.

"Have you heard of Lord Nelson?" Nina asked.

"Yes. There was a pub near our old house in London that was named after him. He was a famous soldier, wasn't he?"

"Not a soldier, no. Nelson was a British naval commander during the Napoleonic wars. He visited the Forest of Dean in 1802 looking for timber to build warships. He was so shocked at how few trees there were that he urged the Admiralty, which was in charge of the Navy, to plant more oaks. Thirty million acorns were planted, but by the time the trees had grown it was too late and ships were being built out of iron and steel."

"So that was a complete and utter waste of time."

"Oh no, I wouldn't say that," said Nina. "If they hadn't planted those millions of acorns we wouldn't have our beautiful forest today. I'm glad they didn't think too far ahead."

Poppy looked at the old oak. Its girth was so wide she doubted that three people could have linked arms around it. "So is this one of the trees Nelson's lot planted?"

"Who knows? But it's certainly hundreds of years old. And it gave the house its name, of course."

Poppy thought for a minute. Something was nagging her. "Aren't acorns poisonous to horses?" she said.

Nina looked impressed. "Yes, they are. So are the leaves. I spend most of the autumn sweeping the yard to make sure there aren't any for the horses to eat. It's hard work. But the tree is so much a part of Oaklands that I don't really mind."

They reached the gate and Nina opened it so Poppy could lead Beau through.

"You must really love this place," Poppy said.

Nina tightened her grip on the gate and Poppy was alarmed to see a look of anguish cross her face.

"Yes," Nina said quietly. "I do."

Poppy decided not to join the others in front of the television after dinner that evening, and instead disappeared into the bedroom to read. She had half hoped that Scarlett would persuade her to stay but instead her friend, who was sitting on the sofa with Cally, had barely thrown her a backward glance. She felt both irritated and dismayed at the way Cally had so effortlessly hijacked her best friend. It was as if Scarlett had been dazzled by the older girl's personality and had forgotten Poppy even existed. Poppy rubbed her aching shoulders and found the latest issue of Young Rider Magazine, which she'd stuffed inside her bag when she'd packed. Her winning story had been published in full along with those of the two runners up. The editor had asked her to email in a photo of her and Cloud, and Poppy had picked her favourite picture, taken by Charlie on his little digital camera a few weeks before. Cloud's silver mane was blowing in the wind and Poppy was laughing as she held a carrot for him in the palm of her hand. *"Great photo!"* the editor had emailed back, and they'd used it above her story. Poppy studied the picture and wondered yet again if Cloud was missing her. There was no mobile phone signal at the house, otherwise she'd have been ringing or texting Caroline several times a day to check he was alright. She didn't like to ask to use the phone at Oaklands unless it was an emergency.

She remembered the last email she'd had from the editor, letting her know when her story would be published. *"Perhaps you'd consider writing a small report on your holiday for us to publish in a future edition,"* she had added.

"Hmph," said Poppy as she switched on the

bedside light and settled down to read. "I don't suppose Young Rider Magazine is interested in horror stories about pig-headed carthorses."

She tried to concentrate on an in-depth article about dressage but it was no good. Her attention kept wandering. Flinging the magazine down beside the bed she went in search of a glass of water. As she passed the door to the lounge she glanced in and saw Scarlett and the others laughing uproariously at a sitcom. It was one of Poppy's favourite programmes but she felt too left out of things to join them. Instead she carried on towards the kitchen, trying to ignore the loneliness that had been her constant companion since they'd arrived at Oaklands.

The kitchen was in darkness, the only light coming from the digital clock on the oven and the red flashing light of the answerphone. Not bothering to turn on the light Poppy headed for the larder, where Nina kept the glasses, mugs and plates. She opened the old wooden door and was reaching up for a tumbler when she heard footsteps. Suddenly the room was flooded with light. Poppy froze. Nina had told them they should help themselves to drinks but she felt awkward skulking around in the dark. She realised it was Nina, humming to herself as she filled the kettle. Poppy was about to breeze out with a glass in her hand when she heard the click of the answerphone and a man's voice filled the air.

To sidle out now would seem suspicious so Poppy crept to the furthest corner of the larder, squeezing between a sack of potatoes and a shelf stacked with saucepans and baking tins.

"This is a message for Nina Goddard of Oaklands Trekking Centre," the man announced in an officious tone.

Nina stopped humming. Even from the depths of the larder Poppy could sense the tension in the air.

"My name is Graham Deakins and I am a financial asset investigation specialist," he continued. Poppy caught Nina's sharp intake of breath.

"I need to talk to you urgently about monies due. Please phone me at your earliest convenience on -" Nina cut the man off mid-sentence. When Poppy heard a small sob she wished she was anywhere but there, witnessing Nina's distress. She breathed as quietly as she could, her heart thudding, until the kitchen light went out and she heard the door close. She didn't know who the man was, or what he wanted. But she knew one thing for certain. It wasn't good news.

The next morning Nina seemed her usual cheerful self and Poppy wondered if she'd misunderstood the answerphone message. To her surprise she managed to catch Beau, groom him and tack him up without being bitten, knocked flying or having her feet stamped on, and felt as though she was making real progress. It was a glorious early summer day and the hedgerows were brimming with frothy-white cow parsley and magenta red campion. The sun was warm on her back and she whistled quietly to herself as she and Beau ambled down the lane behind the others.

They stopped for lunch in a grassy clearing deep in the forest, surrounded by oaks and electric green bracken. They took their sandwiches and drinks from their saddle bags and looped their reins over their horses' heads so they could hold them while they ate. Poppy's stomach was rumbling and she wolfed down her squashed cheese and pickle sandwich in seconds. Beau's head fell, his eyes closed and before long he was fast asleep, his bottom lip drooping unattractively. Poppy took a swig of her water and listened to the conversations going on around her. Chloe and Jess were debating the merits of cross country over showjumping and Jack was telling Nina about his latest computer game. Although she was giving a good impression of being interested, there was a vacant look in her eyes and her mind was obviously elsewhere. Scarlett was quizzing Cally about the latest ex-racehorse she was re-training.

"We think she has great potential as an eventer. I'm working on her dressage at the moment then Rose says I can enter her in her first one day event. They fetch more money if they've started competing."

"That's so cool," Scarlett said. "Maybe I could come and watch."

Poppy tutted to herself and yawned. Rays of sunlight piercing the heavy oak leaves lit yellow celandines and waxy white wood anemones on the forest floor like tiny spotlights illuminating characters on a theatre stage. She leant against the bough of a tree and watched Beau dozing until her own eyelids felt heavy. Before long she, too, was asleep.

She was woken by a gentle nudge on her shoulder and opened her eyes to see Beau's hairy face centimetres from her own. His warm breath smelt of spring grass and his whiskers tickled her cheek. The others were gathering up their lunch things and Poppy jumped to her feet and pulled on her hat. She found a tree stump to use as a mounting block and sprang into the saddle. Steering Beau over to Topaz and Scarlett she said lightly, "Hello stranger. How's things?"

"Great, I'm having a fantastic time. Topaz's brilliant. I'm going to miss her so much," said Scarlett passionately. Poppy pictured Blaze, her friend's loyal Dartmoor pony, grazing in her field back home.

Scarlett guessed what she was thinking. "I love Blaze, of course I do, but I've almost outgrown her, Poppy, you know that. You've got Cloud waiting for you at home. Imagine how ridiculous I'll look on Blaze when we ride out together. I wish Mum and Dad would buy Topaz."

"But she's not for sale, Scar. Nina needs her for the riding holidays. She'll be someone else's pony next week." When Poppy saw the hurt on her best friend's face she could have kicked herself for being so tactless, but it was too late to take the words back. She wasn't surprised when Scarlett resumed her place

beside Cally, leaving her on her own behind Jack,
staring at Rocky's chestnut hindquarters yet again.

They passed a farm. "That's where my nearest
neighbours, Bert and Eileen, live," Nina told them. "I
have permission to ride on their land. We'll be going
through the farmyard and then we'll cross the river
and follow the line of trees back home."

"Are we going to ride through the river?" asked
Jess, her eyes wide.

"Heavens, no," laughed Nina, as they reached the
gate to the yard. "There's an old stone clapper bridge.
We'll ride over that. I'll open the gate. Who's going to
close it for me?"

"I will," said Poppy, and they all looked around in
surprise, as if they'd forgotten she was there.

"If you're sure," said Nina.

"Of course," replied Poppy. She'd never actually
opened a gate while riding - Scarlett always did that -
but, honestly, how hard could it be? Poppy kicked
Beau through the gate after the others and hauled him
to a halt. He stood perfectly still. The only trouble
was, they were just out of reach of the gate. She
squeezed her legs. He ignored her. She exhaled loudly
and booted him in the sides. The cob took a step
sideways. Poppy leant over his shoulder, puffing as
she strained to reach the latch. Her hand tightened
around the iron post and she kicked again. Beau took
another reluctant step forward. She was millimetres
away from setting the latch in its keeper. She leant
even further out of the saddle, her arms stretched taut

as she lunged for the gatepost.

Beau, bored of waiting, took a step backwards. And then another. Poppy teetered for a nano-second but it was no good. With the inevitability of night following day, she slid to the ground and landed, backside first, into a freshly-laid cow pat.

CHAPTER 8

Things went from bad to worse when they arrived
back at the yard and Nina announced that they were
going to spend the rest of the afternoon playing
gymkhana games.

"I'll split you into two teams of three and we'll have
our own Prince Philip Cup competition," she said.
Jack whooped and Chloe and Jess high-fived each
other. Scarlett was also smiling. Poppy pictured the
back of Scarlett's bedroom door, which was plastered
with the many rosettes she and Blaze had won at local
gymkhanas. Cally looked unimpressed, her mouth
turned down in disdain. At fourteen and about to
compete in her first one day event on a former
racehorse, she was obviously way too cool for
gymkhana games. Poppy looked at Beau in despair.
How on earth was she supposed to navigate the great
oaf around bending poles at high speed when she

could barely get him to break into a trot down a straight country lane? It would be yet another opportunity for some ritual humiliation.

Nina untacked McFly and turned him out with Frank in the top field and then opened the gate into the smaller paddock behind the hay barn. It was a flat, square field surrounded by hedges and in the middle were two sets of five evenly-spaced poles set in rows in the ground. Traffic cones marked the start. The children followed Nina in.

"Jack and Scarlett, you can be my two captains, and I'll let you take it in turns to pick your teams," said Nina. Brilliant, thought Poppy with relief. At least Scarlett would pick her.

"Ladies first," said Jack, and Scarlett nodded her thanks. She glanced at Poppy, her face inscrutable. Poppy had a horrible feeling she knew what was coming next.

"Cally," Scarlett said, and Poppy squirmed. It was obviously payback time for being so thoughtless. Cally smiled sweetly at Poppy and rode over to Scarlett's side.

"Jess," Jack said.

"Thanks Jack!" said Jess, surprised and delighted to be her brother's first choice.

Scarlett looked from Chloe to Poppy and back again. Poppy's heart sank. She didn't need to be Einstein to work out who Scarlett was going to pick.

"Chloe, please," said her best friend, avoiding Poppy's gaze.

"I suppose I'd better have Poppy, then," said Jack. Poppy's face was expressionless as she kicked Beau into a trot and joined Jess and Willow.

"Jack's brilliant at gymkhana games," Jess whispered. "He and Magic were picked for our pony club's mounted games team a couple of years ago. He's really competitive."

"Great," Poppy replied, forcing a smile.

"We'll start with a bending race," Nina called. "Captains can decide who races who. I'll give you two points for every win and one point for second place. We'll add all the points up at the end and the winning team gets to have a free evening. The losing team must do evening stables. All clear? Right, who's first?"

Scarlett and Jack both rode up to the starting line beside Nina.

"On your marks, get set, go!" she shouted and Rocky and Topaz set off at a canter. Jack was all arms and legs as he spurred Rocky on, reminding Poppy of a human windmill. The liver chestnut cob valiantly thundered around the poles as fast as he could but couldn't keep up with Topaz. The palomino darted around the poles like a minnow through seaweed and won by a couple of lengths. Scarlett punched the air, her face flushed, and Cally and Chloe cheered.

Jess and Cally were next. Blue was totally over-excited and crabbed over to the starting line, her rose grey neck arched and her tail carriage high. Cally sat quietly in the saddle as the Arab mare danced beneath her. Poppy could hear her murmuring to Blue. Willow stood placidly, her dun ears pricked. Jess looked distinctly green.

Nina started the race and the two girls set off. Although Blue was by far the faster horse she overshot the turns and Cally struggled to keep her balance. In contrast Willow cantered steadily around the poles and turned tightly at the top and by the time they both crossed the finish line they were neck and neck.

"Photo finish!" yelled Jack.

Nina, who had been scrutinising the finish as closely as a line judge at Wimbledon, straightened her back. "Sorry Jack, the budget doesn't run to cameras. I'm going to call it a dead heat and give both teams two points. So Scarlett's team are still in the lead by a point. Chloe and Poppy, you're next."

Poppy pushed her hat firmly down over her forehead and gathered her reins. Beau's head was hanging low and she had the horrible feeling he'd fallen asleep again.

"Come on, Beau," she said firmly and gave him a none-too-gentle kick. The piebald cob's head shot up in surprise and he trotted obediently over to the start line. Poppy was cheered. Maybe they wouldn't make a show of themselves. Maybe Beau was an old pro at this kind of thing. But as she lined up beside Chloe and Rusty, Nina gave her a sympathetic smile. "I'm afraid gymkhana games aren't really Beau's thing, Poppy. Do the best you can."

"Great," Poppy muttered again, glancing over at

Scarlett and Cally. The amused expression on Cally's face hardened her heart and she whispered in Beau's hairy ear, "Let's show them we mean business, eh?"

"Ready?" asked Nina. Both girls nodded. "On your marks, get set, GO!"

Beau gave a giant cat leap forward, almost unseating Poppy, and she grabbed the pommel of the saddle as he cantered towards the first pole. Rusty and Chloe were streaking ahead and she crouched low over Beau's neck and hauled him around the first pole with brute strength. She could hear his hooves as they cantered around the next two poles, but her eyes were fixed on the furthest pole. She knew the race could be won by a close turn at the top. Miraculously, Beau executed a perfect flying change as they turned for the final pole and suddenly they were half a length in front of Chloe and Rusty. As they headed back towards the finish line at a gallop, Poppy looked over her shoulder to reassure herself they really were winning. But as she did she dropped the reins a fraction and Beau thundered straight past a pole. Poppy tried to slow him down so they could turn back and go around it but it was no good. Beau's blood was up and he was unstoppable. He gained even more ground on Chloe and Rusty and by the time they crossed the finish line he was three lengths ahead. He slowed down to a walk and snorted in pleasure, thinking he'd won. Poppy stroked his black and white neck automatically and kept her head down to avoid Jack's furious stare.

"Sorry Poppy, I'll have to disqualify you. Beau missed three of the poles," Nina told her.

"I know. But it wasn't Beau's fault. It was mine." Poppy could have kicked herself for losing concentration.

"Cheer up," Nina said. "It's not all bad. Beau turned on a sixpence at the top and I've never seen him do a flying change before. Maybe you'll have more luck in the walk, trot, canter and run."

As it was Nina's optimism was misguided and Poppy didn't win a single race. Cally and Blue notched up a victory in the walk, trot, canter and run, the fourteen-year-old covering the ground on the final leg in easy strides. Scarlett and Jack fought hard for first place in the flag race, but the hours Jack had spent training with his pony club's mounted games team paid dividends and he won by a head. Jess proved to have a steady hand and was a demon in the egg and spoon race. Poppy tripped over her feet and landed face down in the grass in the sack race. Her temper was frayed and her nerves frazzled by the time Nina announced the last game.

"We'll finish with a relay race. Scarlett, your team is only one point ahead, so if you win this you have the evening off. If you don't you'll tie and you'll do evening stables together. I don't have batons so just high-five each other instead. Best of luck everyone."

Jack beckoned Jess and Poppy over for a team talk. "Jess, you're going to go first. Push Willow as fast as she'll go but don't overshoot. You need to make your turn as tight as possible. Poppy, you go next. Just try not to get disqualified, OK? I'll try to make up the time you've lost. Got that? Come on, let's give it our best shot."

Poppy scowled and turned Beau for the start line. Jess and Chloe set off at a gallop, their ponies' manes streaming behind them as they disappeared towards the far pole. Willow was the fastest around the pole and Jess was grinning as she galloped back down towards Poppy. Poppy gathered her reins in her left hand and high-fived Jess with her right. Beau sprang into action, his ears back and his head stretched forward as he charged for the far pole. Poppy turned him tightly and headed for home. She didn't dare look around to see where Cally was. Rocky, standing at the start line, registered Beau's great bulk bowling towards him like a black and white tornado and recoiled backwards. Jack kicked him on, his right arm held aloft ready to high-five her, but the chestnut cob refused to move.

Catching a glimpse of Cally and Scarlett high-fiving, Poppy pointed Beau towards Rocky and kicked.

"Hold him still, you twit!" she shouted to Jack, as Beau motored on like an equine steamroller. She stood up in her stirrups, leant over and slapped Jack's palm as hard as she could. He winced in pain and Rocky sprang away from Beau and towards the far pole. Poppy swung around in the saddle in time to see Scarlett cantering sedately over the finish line, Jack miles behind her.

"Well done, Poppy. You really showed them how it's done," said Jack, as he and Rocky passed her on their way back to the stables.

"Hold on a minute," Poppy replied furiously. "You were the one who couldn't keep your horse still. It wasn't my fault."

"Yes it was. You and Beau are as useless as each other. And now I've got to spend all evening mucking out. Thanks for nothing."

Poppy's resentment simmered as she, Jess and Jack silently worked their way through evening stables. It started to bubble during dinner and by the time they all sat down to watch television it had reached boiling point. She had made up her mind. She was going to find Nina and ask her to swap Beau for another horse. She would point out that she was a competition winner, after all, so should expect a decent ride. In fact, she had a good mind to email the editor of Young Rider Magazine to complain about the fact that she'd been given the worst horse in the yard.

Poppy had no intention of kicking Scarlett off Topaz. Her best friend was barely talking to her as it was. Anyway, there was no need. Cally the expert rider was apparently so experienced in tackling problem horses that it made sense for her to take Beau on and give Blue to Poppy. It was a no brainer.

Nina had disappeared after putting Lydia to bed. Poppy followed the hallway in the opposite direction

to the guest rooms and lounge. The first door she
came to was slightly ajar. Light seeped through into
the hall and she could hear the murmur of a
television. Through the crack between the door and
its frame she saw Nina sitting at a paper-strewn desk,
her back to the door and her head in her hands.
Poppy knocked gently.

There was a pause. Poppy stood awkwardly, unsure
whether to knock again.

"Come in," Nina said eventually. Poppy pushed
open the door and Nina swivelled her chair around.
"Oh Poppy, it's you."

When Poppy saw Nina's blotchy face all thoughts
of Beau disappeared. "Are you OK?" she asked in
alarm.

"Not really, no. But it's nothing for you to worry
about." Nina's voice was wobbly.

"What's happened? Is it Lydia?"

"No, thank goodness. Lydia is fine." Nina ran a
hand across her forehead in an effort to compose
herself and pointed to the well-worn armchair next to
her desk. "Have a seat. What did you want to talk to
me about?"

"Something's wrong, I know it is," Poppy said. But
Nina didn't answer. She was staring blankly at the
portable television in the corner of the room. The ten
o'clock news had started and the newsreader was
talking about the latest Government re-shuffle. Poppy
glanced at the reproduction mahogany desk. There
were four drawers on each side and a green leather

inlaid top, which was almost completely hidden by credit card and bank statements, brown envelopes and bills.

"Nina -" Poppy persisted.

Jolted back into the present Nina scooped the paperwork into one untidy pile and attempted to straighten it into some kind of order. She stood up and pulled the heavy damask curtains closed. Poppy took the opportunity to scan the top statement. There was a jumble of numbers set out in columns. By stretching her neck she could just make out the outstanding balance of four hundred and ninety two pounds. Stamped in red over the top of the statement were two unforgiving words. FINAL REMINDER.

CHAPTER 9

Nina saw Poppy looking at the bills piled in front of her and her face sagged. She looked ten years older.

"Is there a problem?" Poppy asked, gesturing at the paperwork.

"I've just been going through my accounts, that's all."

Poppy pictured the man in the shiny suit who had been so keen to track Nina down. She replayed the answerphone message she'd overheard the night before in her head and everything fell into place.

"It's something to do with that man who was looking for you the other day, isn't it?"

"It's nothing for you to worry about," Nina repeated, sitting down heavily.

Poppy wasn't about to be fobbed off. "Nina, I heard the answerphone message last night. That man who was talking about monies due. I was in the larder getting a glass," she explained, feeling shifty. "I didn't mean to eavesdrop."

Nina was beaten and Poppy saw her chance. "Please tell me what's going on. I might even be able to help."

"No-one can help. It's too late for that." Nina finally met Poppy's eyes. "You really want to know what's wrong?"

Poppy nodded.

"I've fallen behind with the mortgage payments. My credit cards are maxed to the limit. The horses are due to be shod but the farrier is refusing to come because I still haven't paid him for his last visit. And the next feed bill is due any minute. That man who left a message is a debt collector, Poppy. The irony is, I don't even know who he's working for, I owe so many people money."

"Oh, I see."

"I mortgaged myself to the hilt to buy this place, you see. Lydia's dad and I split up when she was a baby. I was so determined to give her an idyllic childhood, growing up around horses, that when I saw this place I had to have it. Perhaps I was overcompensating. Who knows? But I thought it would work. I did all the research and the bank liked my business plan. I've had so much bad luck, Poppy, you wouldn't believe." Nina ran her hand through her hair. She had kept everything bottled up for so long that now the floodgates were open there was no stopping her.

"Early on I discovered that the house had dry rot and both barns needed re-roofing. Then one of the trekking ponies developed navicular and ran up massive vet's bills. Bookings were much slower than I'd predicted and everything has been so much more expensive. I took out credit cards to keep things ticking over but the interest they've been charging me is crippling. The final straw came last week when the bank warned me that it's going to foreclose on my loan if I can't make this month's payment."

Nina buried her head in her hands again. Her fingers were trembling. When she finally spoke, her voice was muffled with tears.

"I'm going to lose it all, Poppy. Everything."

Poppy looked around her helplessly. It was at times like these that she wished she had Scarlett's easy manner, Caroline's natural empathy or her old friend Tory's old-fashioned common sense. She had no idea how to comfort Nina. She stood up and laid a hand gingerly on the woman's shoulders. But Nina had wrapped herself so tightly in her own misery that she didn't even notice.

Poppy nearly jumped out of her skin when she heard her dad's voice behind her. She spun around to see his face staring out from Nina's portable television. She'd forgotten that her dad, a war correspondent for the BBC, had been sent to northern France to cover the anniversary of the D-Day landings. He was interviewing a veteran whose lined face was wet with tears as he remembered the events of June 1944. She could hear the compassion in her dad's voice and wished with all her heart that he was here with her. She glanced at Nina. What would he do, in her shoes? He'd stay level-headed and practical, that's what he'd do. Poppy spied a box of tissues on the window ledge and offered them to Nina, who finally lifted her head, gave her a watery smile and blew her nose noisily.

"Thank-you, Poppy. I shouldn't have burdened you with all this. I was hoping we'd make it to the end of the week before I had to close down the yard, but I've ruined your holiday now anyway."

"No, you haven't," said Poppy, offering Nina another tissue. "Anyway, it's not your fault. You've just been unlucky. Isn't there anything else you could do? Sell off some land or a couple of the ponies, to give you a bit more time?"

"No, it would be too little, too late. Unless I come up with two thousand pounds by the end of the week the house and land will be repossessed by the bank and I'll probably be declared bankrupt. It'll be down to the bailiffs to sell the horses, and they're not going to care whether they go to good homes or not. How will I tell Lydia that we're moving, let alone that she's going to lose Frank? He and Beau were the first horses I bought for the business, that's why I'm so fond of them both. They've been my talismans from day one, although they don't seem to have brought me much luck recently."

Poppy remembered why she had sought Nina out and felt immensely relieved that she hadn't added to her troubles by complaining about the piebald cob. She could kick herself for being so petty and self-centred. She gave Nina the box of tissues. "I'm going to make you a cup of tea. You sit and watch the end of the news. I won't be long."

Nina was watching the weather when Poppy let herself back into the study, a mug of tea in each hand. The map of the UK was awash with black clouds and lightning symbols.

"Uh oh. Are we in for a storm?" she asked.

Nina had used the short time while Poppy was in the kitchen to collect herself and her voice was almost back to normal.

"Yes, I'm afraid so. The Met Office has issued severe weather warnings for tomorrow night. We're getting the tail-end of a hurricane that hit the Caribbean last week, apparently."

"So our last night might go out with a bang, then?" said Poppy, attempting to raise a smile. Nina nodded bleakly.

Scarlett was already in the top bunk when Poppy let herself into their bedroom.

"Scar, are you awake?" she whispered. Scarlett's shoulders were stiff and her shallow breathing wasn't the rhythmic inhale, exhale of someone fast asleep. But she didn't reply.

Poppy sighed. She would have liked to have talked

to her best friend about Nina's revelations. As Poppy had left the study Nina had asked her not to say anything about her money troubles to the others. But Poppy always shared everything with Scarlett.

At least she always had.

CHAPTER 10

Scarlett was nowhere to be seen when Poppy arrived for breakfast. Everyone else was sat around the table, plates of toast in front of them. Nina hadn't touched hers and her face was pale but she gave Poppy a wide smile.

"Has anyone seen Scarlett?" Poppy asked.

"She said she didn't feel like breakfast. I think she's in the yard," said Chloe.

Poppy bolted down two slices of toast. "Thanks Nina. I'm going to go and find her if that's OK? What time are we setting off?"

"Ten o'clock. I've got an extra special route planned for today."

Frank met Poppy at the back door and followed her across the yard to Topaz's loose box. She hesitated outside. Scarlett was talking to Topaz as she groomed the palomino mare. Poppy knew eavesdropping only led to trouble but she couldn't help herself.

" - I'm going to miss you so much. I've had such a great holiday. I wish Mum and Dad had the money to buy you. You'd love it at Ashworthy." Poppy heard a sob. She reached into her pocket for a tissue and let herself into Topaz's box. Scarlett was standing with her arms around the mare, her shoulders shuddering. Poppy had never seen her friend cry.

"Have this," she said, handing Scarlett the tissue.

"Oh, it's you." Scarlett looked far from pleased to see her.

Poppy took a deep breath. "I'm sorry I was so thoughtless yesterday, I really am. I didn't realise how much Topaz meant to you."

Scarlett was silent. Poppy persisted. "I know I haven't been much fun to be around and I don't blame you for hanging out with Cally. But I've missed you, Scar. Please forgive me so we can be friends again."

Scarlett sniffed and wiped her face on the sleeve of her sweatshirt. She ran her hand down Topaz's neck and looked at Poppy coolly.

"You're doing it again. Me, me, me. You have to remember that it's not all about you, Poppy. At least Cally is interested in what I think and how I feel. She doesn't just go on about herself all the time."

Poppy was stung. "Yes she does!" she said indignantly. "If she's not boring the pants off us with stories about what a good rider she is she's going on about how popular she is at school. She never stops talking about herself. And you encourage her by hanging onto her every word like some kind of saddo."

"How dare you! At least I'm not always feeling sorry for myself. Some people would give their eye teeth to be given a horse like Beau for a week and all you've done is whinge and moan since the minute we arrived."

"You ought to try riding the lumbering great brute before being so quick to judge. My legs are killing me, and as for my back -"

"There you go again!" Scarlett exploded. "You just can't see it, can you?"

Poppy bit her bottom lip as Scarlett turned her back to her, picked up a body brush and started sweeping it over Topaz's golden flank.

"I'm going then, seeing as you obviously can't stand my company any more," she said, hoping Scarlett would dissolve into giggles and tell her that she was only kidding and that Poppy would always be her best friend.

But she didn't.

Instead she said tonelessly, "Suit yourself."

Poppy, shaken by the indifference in Scarlett's voice, let herself out of the loose box, almost colliding with Beau, who was making a beeline for the hay barn.

"How on earth did you get out?" she cried, grabbing his headcollar. As she did she saw a car pull up the track. It was the silver saloon. Poppy stood and watched as the driver's door swung open and the man in the shiny suit emerged. He saw her and beckoned her over. Poppy glanced at the back door of the bungalow. Nina must still be clearing up their breakfast things. She strode purposefully towards him, dragging Beau behind her.

"Oh, it's you," he said, echoing Scarlett. No-one seemed pleased to see her today. Poppy nodded, noticing with satisfaction that his suit was still peppered with flecks of dried snot.

"Before you ask, Nina's not here," she told him, her voice hostile.

The man looked pained. "Do you know when she'll be back?"

Poppy shrugged. "No idea."

He reached inside his jacket. "Here's my card. Give it to her and tell her to call me, will you? It's vital that I speak to her and the sooner the better. Do you understand?"

Poppy grunted, stuffed the card deep into her pocket and pulled Beau back towards the barn. She sneaked a look over her shoulder as she tied him up but the car had disappeared down the long, bumpy track.

CHAPTER 11

For once Poppy was glad of Beau's snail's pace, which put a welcome distance between her and the others as they headed down the lane towards the forest. It gave her head space to analyse the row with Scarlett. Poppy wasn't blind to her own faults. She knew she'd been thoughtless. And maybe she had gone on a bit about Beau. But she also felt aggrieved. Scarlett had virtually ignored her ever since they'd arrived at Oaklands. When Poppy had said sorry her best friend had thrown the apology back in her face. And then she'd had the nerve to say it was Poppy's fault for being self-obsessed. She wished Caroline was with her so she could talk it over, but as there was no mobile phone signal at the house she couldn't even give her stepmum a call.

She looked down at Beau's tufty black ears, which were pointing resolutely ahead as he followed the others down a narrow bridleway that wound its way through beech trees. As Nina had handed them their sandwiches she'd told them they were heading deep into the forest for their last ride of the holiday, and that they were to keep their eyes peeled for fallow deer and wild boar.

"What do you think about it all, Beau?" The piebald cob flicked back an ear at the sound of her voice. She talked all the time to Cloud, she realised guiltily. There was no reason she shouldn't talk to Beau, too. "Is it my fault, or Scarlett's fault? Or is it six to one and half a dozen to the other? I wish I knew."

The path opened out into a plantation of imposing pine trees whose gnarly trunks soared high into the sky. The air was warm and still and there was no sign of the storm the weather forecaster had predicted the night before. A grey squirrel darted down one of the trees head first and paused at the bottom where it eyed Poppy and Beau warily. Scarlett temporarily forgotten, Poppy tugged at Beau's reins and they stopped to watch the squirrel streak across the path in front of them and up a tree on the opposite side. It settled on a branch above their heads and began nibbling on a pine cone, its whiskers twitching and its tail wrapped around its back like an inverted question mark. Tired of the pine cone the squirrel discarded it and it fell to the forest floor like a stone. Beau, who had been nibbling on a patch of grass, walked over to the cone and snorted loudly, making Poppy laugh. The squirrel froze at the sound and vanished through the leaf-laden branches. Poppy picked up her reins and looked along the path for Rocky's chestnut rump. But it had disappeared from sight.

"Great, they've gone without us." They picked up a trot until they reached a fork in the path and Poppy pulled Beau up. "Left or right?" she pondered. Beau took a step towards the left-hand fork, which climbed steadily through the conifers. "No Beau, I think it's this way," she told him, turning him down the path to their right.

When twenty minutes had passed and there was no sign of the others Poppy began to doubt her wisdom. She should have trusted Beau. He'd probably been on this ride dozens of times. She'd just decided to cut her losses and turn back the way they'd come when she heard hooves pounding behind them. Cally was cantering up on Blue, her face like thunder.

"There you are!" the older girl said in exasperation. "Nina sent me to find you. The others are way ahead. How on earth did you end up here?"

"We must have taken a wrong turn," said Poppy. "Sorry."

Cally exhaled loudly. "We'd better cut the corner to catch them up, otherwise we'll be here all day."

She steered Blue off the path and Beau and Poppy followed them into bracken so tall it skimmed their stirrups. Under the canopy of green fronds the ground was broken and uneven. Almost as though it had been turned by a rotavator like the one Caroline had hired to dig over her vegetable patch when they'd first moved to Riverdale. Although why someone would want to plant vegetables in the middle of the forest was beyond Poppy. Beau tripped over a mound of freshly-turned earth, forcing Poppy forwards as his nose almost touched the ground.

"Steady on, Beau," she said, pulling his head back up. Cally shot her a disparaging look. Even Blue flicked her silky tail with derision. Poppy pulled a face at them and patted the cob's neck. "I'd ignore them if I were you," she said to him under her breath.

The bracken was by now virtually impenetrable and Poppy was about to question Cally on the wisdom of her short cut when she heard a rustle to their left. Beau stopped and stared intently into the undergrowth, his ears flicking back and forth. Poppy clicked her tongue and squeezed firmly with her legs.

"Come on Beau, it's just a rabbit or something. Walk on," she instructed. But the cob was deaf to her aids and stood rooted to the spot, his nostrils flared.

Cally spun Blue around. Her face was a mask of irritation. "What's wrong now?"

As she spoke, the bracken rippled and the russet head of a tiny animal poked out. It had a black snout and vertical dark stripes ran along the length of its body.

Poppy couldn't believe her luck. A wild boar piglet! Beau was stock still beneath her and she stroked his neck to calm him. She watched, enthralled, as three more piglets joined the first and began snouting around in the long grass a few metres from where they stood.

Blue began backing out of the bracken, snorting with fear.

"They won't hurt you, you silly horse, they're tiny," Cally said, kicking her on. "Come on, Poppy, we really need to go."

But the highly-strung Arab was trembling with fear. She had seen something far more dangerous than a litter of wild boar piglets thrusting its way through the undergrowth. Poppy gasped as an enormous sow, ready to defend her young, burst through the bracken with an angry squeal.

In the split second before the wild boar charged Poppy registered her bright black eyes and thick, bristly black coat. The boar had short, stocky legs and a powerful body with a ridge of coarse long hair along her spine, like a raven-haired punk with a Mohican. Her head low, she hurled herself towards them, scattering the piglets in her wake. Poppy gripped her reins and prepared to turn and gallop. But Beau stood his ground. She felt his strength beneath her, so solid and utterly dependable, and suddenly knew what they had to do. Kicking Beau into a canter she took a deep breath and began yelling at the top of her voice. She stood up in her stirrups and waved her arms in the air as they thundered towards the sow.

After ten years' living wild in the forest the boar knew which fights to pick and when to give in gracefully. The sight of a black and white, blue-eyed beast with a screaming banshee on board galloping hell for leather towards her was enough to stop her in her tracks. She slid to a halt, her snout quivering, and turned and fled back through the wall of bracken.

Poppy whooped, her adrenalin levels sky high, and swivelled around to Cally. The older girl was struggling to control Blue. The sight of the boar had sent the mare into a blind panic. Her ears were flattened and Poppy could see the whites of her eyes. She was spinning around like a pirouetting ballerina. Cally tugged at Blue's reins in an attempt to steady her but it only seemed to terrify her more. The mare's head shot up and her muscles tensed as her instinct for flight took hold.

Poppy saw Blue shift her weight onto her hindquarters and knew with dread what was going to happen before the mare's front feet left the ground.

"Lean forward! She's going to rear!" she shouted. Cally shot a frightened glance in her direction as Blue stood on her back legs, waving her forelegs wildly in the air.

"Wrap your arms around her neck! She's losing her balance!"

Time slowed down as the panic-stricken mare thrashed about in the bracken. Cally had lost a stirrup and was fighting to keep her own balance. Poppy pushed Beau forwards. Maybe if they got close enough she could grab Blue's reins and stop her rearing. They were within a few tantalising feet when Blue stumbled on an old tree trunk on the forest floor that was so green with lichen it was almost invisible.

The last thing Poppy heard as Blue somersaulted backwards was Cally's scream as she landed with a sickening crash in the bracken.

CHAPTER 12

Blue picked herself up, tossed her dished head and galloped away through the pine trees, her reins and mane flying. Poppy dithered for a few seconds, unsure whether to follow the mare or stay with Cally. The sound of the older girl groaning spurred her into action. She scrambled off Beau and ran towards the noise. Cally was sitting on her haunches at the base of a tree, cradling her head in her hands.

"Are you OK?" Poppy asked urgently.

"What?" Cally looked dazed.

"Did you hit your head when you fell?" Poppy said, crouching down next to her.

"How do I know? Anyway, I'm not worried about that. Where's Blue?"

"She's gone, Cally."

"You're joking. Why didn't you catch her?" Cally stood up shakily and glared at Poppy. When she started swaying Poppy grabbed her elbow and pushed her firmly back down.

"Sit down, for goodness sake. You hold Beau and I'll see if I can find her."

Cally was about to argue when she saw the determined set of Poppy's jaw. She sank back against the tree and took Beau's reins without a quibble. "I can't believe I fell off. What an idiot. And why didn't I hang on to the reins? How on earth am I going to tell Nina I've lost her best trekking pony?" she muttered.

Poppy felt an unwelcome twinge of sympathy. "You won't have to. I don't suppose she's gone far." She ran her hand down Beau's neck and gave Cally a brief smile. "I'll find her, I promise."

Shafts of light played on the acid green bracken as Poppy fought her way through the undergrowth in the direction Blue had disappeared. The smell of earth and decomposing leaf mulch all at once reminded her of the Riverdale wood. Only this time she was looking for Blue and not Cloud and she didn't have Charlie at her side, his face streaked with camouflage paint and a pair of binoculars around his neck as he inspected the ground for big cat paw prints. The seven-year-old would be gutted when he heard he'd missed a close encounter with a whole family of wild boar.

Poppy scanned the trees for any sign of the mare. Cally had looked defeated and much younger than her fourteen years as she'd leant against the trunk of the enormous pine tree. Her bravado, the over-confidence Poppy had found so intimidating from their very first encounter, had completely evaporated. Perhaps it had all been bluster and deep down she was as insecure as Poppy. How ironic that would be.

Broken fronds of bracken brushed Poppy's jodhpurs. When she looked down she realised the vegetation had been trampled and she was following a distinct path through the undergrowth. Her senses on full alert, she heard the mare before she saw her.

"Blue," she called softly. "It's OK, I'm here." Blue was pawing the ground by a fallen tree, her reins entangled in the branches, her neck dark with sweat. Poppy knew that if she startled the mare she could pull back in panic, snap the leather and career off again, her reins dragging dangerously by her feet. She lowered her eyes and inched towards her, talking in a low murmur, just as she had when she'd approached Cloud in the Riverdale wood. She stole a glance at Blue and saw with relief that she had stopped pawing the ground and was watching her curiously, her velvety brown eyes fixed on Poppy. When she was a couple of paces away Poppy reached in her pocket for a Polo and held out her palm. Blue lowered her head and sniffed suspiciously, her muscles tensed. But it gave Poppy enough time to take hold of her reins and untangle them from the branch.

"Come on, girl. Let's get you back to Cally. I think she's going to be pretty pleased to see you."

Poppy considered jumping onto the mare and

cantering back to Cally and Beau. But the prospect of riding the horse she'd hankered after all week had lost its appeal. Suddenly all she wanted was her level-headed cob.

Cally was still sitting with her head in her hands at the base of the pine tree, Beau by her side.

"We're back," Poppy called. "I've checked her over and she looks fine. She hasn't even broken her reins. I'd say you've both had a lucky escape." She pretended not to notice Cally's tear-stained cheeks as she handed Blue's reins back to the older girl. "I'll hold her for you while you get on," she offered.

Cally nodded her thanks and mounted Blue. She looked down at Poppy, her blue-grey eyes appraising.

"That was a really brave thing to do. That wild boar could have attacked you both."

"Oh, I knew Beau would look after me," Poppy replied lightly. "Although I think I may have permanently damaged my vocal chords with all the screaming," she grinned.

Cally was quiet for a while as they headed back through the bracken to the path.

"I think I may have been wrong about you," she said eventually.

"What do you mean?"

"I thought you were stuck-up and standoffish. Poppy the Ice Maiden."

Poppy giggled. "That's funny, because I thought you were a massive show off with an ego the size of

Texas."

"Why Texas?" Cally asked, her mouth twitching.

"Oh, I don't know. It was the first place I thought of. And Texas is pretty big." Poppy paused. "Anyway, I'm not stuck-up, Cally. It's shyness. People always think I'm being unfriendly but I'm really not. I just find meeting new people terrifying. And before I know it they've made up their minds about me. Like you obviously did."

"Maybe you're right," Cally conceded. "Mum's always telling me not to be so quick to judge. Scarlett's so open and friendly. She's the complete opposite of you. I couldn't for the life of me work out how you ended up best friends."

"That's because she didn't give me a chance to be shy." Poppy recalled the day Scarlett had first turned up at Riverdale, her bubbly personality cancelling out Poppy's natural diffidence. Then she remembered that she and Scarlett weren't speaking and looked down at Beau's unruly mane in despair.

"I thought you'd made friends with Scarlett just to annoy me."

"That's so not true," Cally retorted. "I made friends with Scarlett because she's good company and we have a laugh together."

"I see that now. And you've got a good taste in friends. Scarlett's the best," Poppy replied, a catch in her throat.

Cally smiled sympathetically. "You two'll make up, don't worry. If it's any consolation, Scarlett has spent the whole holiday trying to convince me what an amazing person you are."

Poppy found that hard to believe, but it was kind of Cally to say so. "Anyway, now we've decided that I'm not a stuck up ice maiden and you're not a big fat show off, shall we start again? Friends?" she asked.

"Friends," Cally confirmed.

They continued without talking until they saw the others on the brow of a hill. Poppy broke the silence.

"I don't think we should tell Nina what happened back there. Just tell her I'd gone further than you thought."

"Are you sure?"

"Definitely. There's no point worrying her. She's got enough on her plate at the moment."

Cally smiled gratefully. "Thanks, Poppy."

Nina held her finger to her lips as they caught up with the others. They were all staring into the valley below. Poppy and Cally followed their gaze and saw a small herd of fallow deer grazing in front of the next band of woodland. Above them a large bird of prey glided over the clearing, its white body flecked with black.

"A goshawk. Probably a female, judging by the size," whispered Nina. "The females are much bigger than the males. This time of year she'll be hunting for her young. She probably has a nest somewhere nearby."

"What's she hunting for?" asked Poppy.

"She'll catch anything from rabbits and squirrels to

crows and pigeons. She's even powerful enough to kill a pheasant."

They watched the deer grazing and the goshawk soaring high above until the horses started fidgeting.

"Come on, I know the perfect place for our picnic," said Nina, gathering McFly's reins. "We've probably had our wildlife fix for today."

"I wanted to see a wild boar," Jack grumbled to his sister as they followed Nina and McFly back into the trees. "Deer and hawks are alright, but that would have been awesome."

Scarlett, riding beside Cally, was puzzled to see the older girl giving Poppy a conspiratorial smile. She arched her eyebrows in surprise.

"What were you and Poppy grinning about? I thought you couldn't stand each other," she quizzed.

"Oh, it turns out we were wrong and you were right," Cally replied. "I'll tell you all about it over lunch."

CHAPTER 13

All too soon their last ride had come to an end and they were clip-clopping down the lane towards the yard. Although the others were being picked up by their parents before dinner, Poppy's dad had arranged with Nina for her and Scarlett to stay an extra night so he could collect the two girls the following morning on his way back from London.

The yard was a picture of activity as they all dismounted and tied up their horses. Lydia's childminder dropped the four-year-old off and Lydia led Frank around the yard saying goodbye to everyone. Poppy broke away from sponging Beau's sweaty saddle marks to watch people untack and brush down their horses. Chloe looked tearful as she smothered Rusty with kisses. Poppy knew she would be going back to her weekly riding lessons, her yearning for a pony of her own stronger than ever.

Jess's arms were flung around Willow's neck, her face buried in the mare's black mane. Even Jack looked subdued as he said goodbye to Rocky. At least the brother and sister had the elderly Magic waiting for them at home. Cally and Scarlett were swapping mobile phone numbers and email addresses.

"Are you going to miss us, Poppy?" said a high-pitched voice, and she looked around to see Lydia and Frank behind her. The Shetland walked straight up to Beau and started nibbling Poppy's quick release knot.

"Come here, you monster!" commanded Lydia, echoing her mum the day they'd arrived and Frank had been caught in the hay barn. Poppy smiled. Time was so elastic, she thought, as she dipped the sponge in a bucket of water and ran it over Beau's back. In some ways it felt as though they'd only arrived that morning, yet she was already so deeply embedded in the Oaklands routine that she felt as though she'd been there for months.

"Are you?" Lydia repeated.

"Well, I can't wait to see my own pony. And it'll be nice to be home. But do you know what? I will miss you," she said, watching Beau nuzzle Frank's bushy mane. "All of you."

Jess and Jack's mum drove up in a people carrier, and the brother and sister were sent indoors to pack. Chloe's dad was next to arrive. He virtually had to prise the ten-year-old away from Rusty with promises of new jodhpurs and a trip to Olympia. Poppy was saying goodbye to Jess and Chloe when a rusty VW camper van lurched up the track and stopped at the gate. Spray-painted a lurid purple, the van had been so completely plastered in daisy car transfers it looked as though it was suffering from a bad attack of the measles.

A slim blonde woman who could have passed for Cally's older sister sprang out of the driver's side. Her hair was tied in two long plaits and she wore a baggy, hand-knitted jumper in rainbow stripes, a long, faded denim skirt and scuffed brown boots. Poppy remembered Scarlett telling her that Cally's mum was a part-time carer and that they struggled to make ends meet. Cally must have worked hard for months to save up for the few days at Oaklands. Poppy realised how galling it must have been for the older girl when she found out Poppy had won the holiday just for writing a story.

Poppy slipped into the barn and stuck her head over the door of Blue's loose box. Cally was brushing tendrils of bracken from the mare's tail.

"Cally, your mum's here."

Cally looked up, dismayed. "Already?"

"'Fraid so. She's talking to Nina."

Poppy stroked Blue's dished head. "I'm glad we sorted everything out this afternoon."

Cally dropped the dandy brush she'd been using into the box of grooming kit and joined Poppy by the loose box door.

"It's just as well. Scarlett has invited me down to

the farm for a week in the summer holidays. You two can show me around."

"That's if Scarlett is still speaking to me," Poppy said gloomily.

"Don't worry. Apparently these things have a habit of working out. That's the old cliché you trotted out the other day, anyway," Cally grinned.

"Very funny, I'm sure."

Cally handed Poppy the grooming kit, her face suddenly solemn. "Tell my mum I'll be over in a minute. I want to say goodbye to Blue."

Scarlett's hazel eyes were downcast as they said their farewells.

"I'll be down before you know it. You can show me all the best rides on Dartmoor," said Cally, giving her a hug.

Poppy caught the older girl's eye. "Good luck. I hope you find your prizewinning showjumper."

"Yeah, well, you never know." Cally turned to her mum. "I'm going to miss Blue so much. I thought I'd ask Rose for some extra hours so I can start saving for a holiday next year."

Poppy's buoyant mood plummeted. In all the drama she'd forgotten about the debt collector. If Nina was right, Oaklands wouldn't be in business next week, let alone next year. Blue would be sold, along with Topaz, McFly, Rusty, Rocky and the others. She realised with a pang that Frank and Beau would be split up, and she wondered how Beau would cope without his pint-sized alter ego. She glanced at Nina. She was smiling and making small talk with Cally's mum but she looked strained, as though she was carrying the weight of the world on her shoulders. Poppy was full of admiration for her. Despite the fact that her world was about to fall apart, she was holding it all together.

But only just.

CHAPTER 14

Scarlett and Nina were both silent over dinner, wrapped up in their own thoughts. Poppy struggled to keep the conversation going and, once they'd cleared the plates away and stacked the dishwasher, offered to do the final check on the horses so she could escape the oppressive atmosphere.

"That would be great, thanks Poppy. I need to watch the weather forecast," said Nina. Scarlett left the kitchen wordlessly, heading in the direction of the lounge, and Poppy let herself out of the back door. The air was still and silent and the sweet smell of honeysuckle hung heavily. All the horses were in the barn except Frank, who was grazing in the small paddock at the far end of the yard. Poppy could just make out his dark outline under the old oak tree. She pulled open the double doors of the barn, breathing in the familiar smell of warm horse, and walked the length of the barn, running her eyes over each horse and pony until she was satisfied they were all well. The last loose box she reached was Beau's. He was lying in the straw, his feathered legs tucked neatly beneath him and his whiskered chin resting on his knee as he dozed.

Poppy leant on his door, watching his flanks gently rise and fall. As if he sensed her presence, the cob opened his wall eye and whickered. Poppy swung around, assuming Frank must have let himself out of his paddock and followed her in, but the Shetland was nowhere to be seen. A gust of wind blew through the half-open double doors, banging them against the inside wall of the barn. McFly whinnied in alarm and Poppy backtracked to his loose box. The thoroughbred looked fretfully over his door.

"It's OK," she soothed, stroking his nose. "It's just the wind picking up. There's going to be a storm tonight, but you'll be safe in here."

Slate grey clouds had appeared on the horizon by the time Poppy pulled the barn doors closed and as she crossed the yard to the back door of the bungalow a few fat raindrops began to fall. She found Nina in her study, glued to the weather, her face anxious.

"They've upped the severe weather warnings from amber to red," she told Poppy. "Were the horses alright?"

"All present and correct," said Poppy. "The barn doors were rattling in the wind so I've bolted them shut." She stifled a yawn. "I think I might head off to bed. It's been a long day."

"Thank-you, Poppy. I'm going to turn in soon, too. Lydia's bound to have me up in the night. She hates thunder."

Poppy poked her head around the door of the lounge on her way to the bedroom. Scarlett was sitting slouched on one end of the sofa, her feet on the oak coffee table, apparently engrossed in a quiz show. Poppy dithered by the door for a minute, her stomach in knots. Then she came to a decision and marched into the room. Perching on the coffee table, she grabbed the remote control and turned off the television.

"Can we *please* stop fighting now?" she asked. "I'll promise to stop whinging if you promise to stop sulking. Call it quits?"

Scarlett dragged her eyes away from the screen. She was frowning.

"There's something I need to say first," she said.

"Oh, right." Poppy wondered what she'd done wrong now. "What is it?"

"I'm sorry. I'm sorry I've spent so much of the holiday with Cally, especially as I wouldn't even be here if you hadn't invited me. I'm sorry I was so touchy about Topaz. Most of all I'm sorry I didn't accept your apology. I've been a terrible friend and I wouldn't blame you for hating me."

Poppy felt the knots vanish and she grinned. "Scar, you idiot! Of course I don't hate you. I know I've been a pain, too. Let's forget all about it."

"Cally told me what happened this morning. You were really brave, Poppy."

"It wasn't me, it was Beau. When he stood up to the wild boar she realised she'd met her match and scarpered. It wasn't as dangerous as it sounds."

"And Cally says you two have finally made friends."

Poppy smiled sheepishly and sat next to Scarlett. "Yes. It turns out you were right about us both, if you must know. How annoying you must find it, being right all the time."

Scarlett smirked. "You get used to it."

Poppy turned the television back on and soon they were convulsed in giggles, shouting out inane answers to the questions fired at contestants by the heavily spray-tanned quiz show host.

As the credits rolled at the end of the programme Poppy groaned, clutching her sides theatrically. "That was fun, but I suppose we ought to get to bed."

The rain was lashing against their bedroom window by the time they climbed into their bunks. Poppy shivered. It felt more like January than the beginning of June.

"I'm glad we're friends again," said Scarlett.

Poppy pulled her duvet under her chin. "Me too."

"Bet you can't wait to see Cloud."

She wriggled her toes in anticipation. "No, I can't. Let's go out for a ride the minute we get back."

"Good plan. I've enjoyed riding in the forest but do you know what? It's not a patch on Dartmoor," said

Scarlett.

"I agree." Poppy pictured Cloud's pricked grey ears in front of her as they cantered across the moor, past rocky tors and black-faced sheep. She wondered if he'd missed her as much as she'd missed him. The wind battered the walls of the bungalow and she could hear the oak tree creaking. She yawned into the darkness.

"'Night Scarlett."

"'Night Poppy, see you in the morning."

As fate and the weather would have it, they didn't have to wait that long. A rumble of thunder, followed by the sound of Lydia wailing, dragged both girls from their dreams.

Poppy sat up groggily and checked her alarm clock. Ten to two in the morning.

"Did you hear that? It sounded like it was right over our heads," exclaimed Scarlett, swinging her legs over the side of the bunk bed.

Suddenly their room was lit by a flash of lightning which illuminated Scarlett's bare feet as they dangled in front of Poppy's face. Scarlett climbed out of bed and raced to the window.

"Quick, count how many seconds before it thunders. See how far away the storm is," she said.

Together they counted to ten before a long, loud rumble reverberated around the room. "Ten miles," said Scarlett.

"Dad says that's an old wives' tale," Poppy told her.

"He says you need to divide the number of seconds by five."

"Two miles then," said Scarlett impatiently. "I *love* thunderstorms."

"Me too. I'm not sure Lydia would agree with us, though." The four-year-old had ratcheted up her wailing by several decibels and was now howling at the top of her voice. They could hear Nina murmuring as she tried in vain to settle her.

Another flash of lightning rent the inky sky, followed a few seconds later by a clap of thunder.

"It's getting closer!" exclaimed Scarlett. As she spoke they heard a click and the light in the hallway went out. "Uh oh. Power cut."

"I'll ask Nina if she has any candles." Poppy turned to go but before she reached the door the room was lit by a third strobe of lightning, followed immediately by a deafening crack of thunder. There was a flash of yellow and an ominous creak. Scarlett, her forehead pressed against the window, gasped. When she turned to Poppy her face had drained of all colour.

"The lightning's hit the oak tree!" she cried. Poppy ran to the window. They watched, horrified, as flames shot out of the old tree as though someone had fixed a giant Catherine wheel to its trunk. With a terrifying groan the tree sliced in two and toppled into the yard with a thunderous boom. Then everything went quiet.

Poppy and Scarlett clutched each other, their thoughts in sync.

"The horses!" they cried.

CHAPTER 15

Never had Poppy dressed so quickly. Within seconds she was running out of their room, Scarlett on her heels.

"Go and tell Nina what's happened and meet me in the yard," she panted. Scarlett nodded and they sprinted in opposite directions, Poppy heading for the back door, Scarlett towards Lydia's bedroom. Poppy grabbed a heavy duty torch from the hook by the door and pulled on her jodhpur boots and coat, her stomach liquid with fear. She cursed as she fumbled with the lock which stubbornly refused to open. "Come *on*!" she muttered, forcing herself to pause and take a couple of deep breaths before tackling it again. This time the key turned smoothly. She yanked the door open and stared into the dark. Driving rain was coming down in sheets, soaking her to the skin in seconds. Remembering the torch, she flicked it on and followed the beam towards the yard.

The scene that greeted her was like the set of a disaster movie abandoned halfway through filming. The lightning strike had cut the oak in two with a surgeon's precision. One half of the tree had crashed into the hay barn, taking the electricity and phone lines with it. The other half had sheared off and fallen in front of the barn where the horses were stabled, blocking the barn doors and the gate to the drive.

Poppy could hear a horse's frantic neighing over the sound of the rain bouncing off the concrete. She ran over to the doors but a huge branch barred her way. She lowered her shoulder to it and pushed with all her strength, but it was immovable.

"Poppy!"

She looked up at the sound of Nina's voice. She was holding a hysterical Lydia in her arms, Scarlett beside her. All three were drenched. Poppy ducked under the branches and made her way over to them.

"The tree's blocking the barn door. I've tried moving it but it's stuck fast," she told them.

"The horses'll be safe in there though, won't they?" asked Scarlett.

"They should be. The roof's fine, although the same can't be said for the hay barn," said Poppy.

Lydia lifted her head from her mum's shoulder and stared at the roof of the hay barn. "More lightning!" she howled, burying her face in Nina's neck.

They spun around. Poppy felt her blood run cold. The electricity cable severed by the tree was arcing wildly like a demented serpent, the end of it glowing as blindingly white as a magnesium flame in a school science lab. They watched, horrified, as it hissed and fizzed, metres away from the barn full of tinderbox dry hay.

"We need to call the fire brigade!" Scarlett shouted to Nina over the wind and rain.

"We can't! The phone line's down and there's no mobile signal here. And I can't get the jeep out - the tree's blocking the gate." Nina's voice was shaky.

"There must be something we can do. How far is the nearest house?" shouted Poppy.

"Three miles away. It's the farm we rode past the other day," Nina reminded them. It seemed like a lifetime ago. "It'll take almost an hour to walk there, especially in this weather."

Poppy looked helplessly at Scarlett and then back at the electricity cable twitching and jumping on the roof of the hay barn. Lydia lifted her tear-streaked face again and peered over her mum's shoulder. "Frank!" she sobbed.

"He'll be OK, he's in the paddock," Nina soothed, stroking her sodden hair.

"No, Mum! He's here!" she cried, pointing into the dark. The Shetland stepped into the beam of the torch and Lydia wriggled out of her mum's arms and ran to him.

"Wait - who's that behind him?" said Poppy. She raised the torch and her heart gave a funny little skip. A hairy face with a forelock like rats' tails, a pink nose and a blue eye staring dolefully at them emerged before their eyes like a mirage.

"Beau! How on earth -" Nina spluttered.

"Frank must have escaped from the paddock and let Beau out of the barn before the tree came down," said Scarlett.

Poppy found herself taking two steps forward. The cob whickered and she flung her arms around his neck. She became aware of Nina talking.

" - and I think it should be you, Poppy."

"What should be me?"

"You need to ride Beau to the farm to get help. I can't leave Lydia, not when she's in this state."

"What about his tack?" Poppy knew without looking that they couldn't get into the tack room - a branch the size of a small tree pinned the door shut. "He hasn't even got a headcollar on."

"I've got a spare headcollar in the house. It's a bit small but it'll do. Scarlett, it's hanging on the coat stand in the hallway. Will you run and get it?"

Scarlett nodded and raced towards the house.

Poppy still wasn't sure. "I've never ridden bareback before. What if I can't stay on?"

"You'll be fine. Beau'll look after you. Head for the far end of the top field, turn left after you've gone through the gate and follow the line of trees for a couple of miles until you get to the clapper bridge. The farm's straight ahead. Tell Bert and Eileen what's happened and get them to call the fire brigade. Even if their phone line's down I think they get a mobile signal there."

Scarlett appeared beside them and thrust the headcollar and a frayed leadrope into Poppy's hands. She tried to unfasten the buckle on the headpiece but her fingers were so cold they wouldn't work properly. Scarlett grabbed the headcollar back, slipped it on and fastened the buckle. She clipped the leadrope to the ring on one side, tied the end to the ring on the other and handed the makeshift reins to Poppy, who took them reluctantly.

"I think Scarlett should go. She's a much better rider than me," she stalled.

"Beau trusts you, Poppy. Just look at him," said Scarlett. Poppy realised the cob had edged towards her and was nuzzling her hand, his breath warming her freezing fingers, his pink nose as soft as velvet.

Nina broke the silence. "Listen, we haven't got time to argue. I'll give you a leg up."

Still Poppy was rooted to the spot.

Scarlett bellowed in her ear. "Hurry up Poppy! I couldn't bear it if something happened to Topaz."

The thought of the horses trapped in the barn while the deadly electricity cable was writhing unrestrained a few feet away finally brought her to her senses. She ran around to Beau's near side, put her knee in Nina's cupped hands and grabbed a handful of Beau's mane.

"On the count of three," Nina shouted. "One...two...three!" Nina pushed Poppy skywards and she flung her right leg over Beau's back, landing with a jolt. Nina passed her the makeshift reins and she took a hank of mane in each hand and wound it around her fingers.

Nina took a step back. "So you know where you're going?"

Poppy nodded. "I think so."

"You'll have to ride around the back of the barn and over the muck heap. It's the only way out. Good luck. And stay safe."

Poppy gave the ghost of a smile and clicked her tongue.

"Come on Beau. Let's go."

CHAPTER 16

They trotted out of the yard towards the muck heap, a horseshoe-shaped construction with old railway sleepers stacked five feet high on three sides and piled high with manure. Beau paused at the bottom and Poppy squeezed her legs. "Come on boy, up you go." With a grunt he sprang from his hindquarters to the top of the heap. Poppy gasped as she felt herself sliding backwards. She baulked at the sheer drop down the other side of the sleepers to the field but Beau had no such hesitation. He leapt over the edge, landing heavily on the saturated ground. The impact threw Poppy forwards and she clutched his neck, clinging on like ivy. Beau lifted his head, tipping her upright again, and she tightened her grip on the leadrope.

The rain pelted down, gluing her eyelashes together, and she leant forwards and wiped her face on her arm. She knew she had to cross the field diagonally to the gate at the far end but in the dark it was impossible to see where it was. She just had to guess. She kicked Beau into a canter and within seconds he was loping along, his long, rocking-horse strides eating up the ground. She urged him faster and he extended his stride into a gallop. Without thinking Poppy adopted a jockey's position, crouching low over the cob's outstretched neck, her hair plastered to her face.

After a while Beau slowed to a canter and then broke into a trot. Poppy could just make out the shadow of the post and rail fence that marked the end of Nina's land. She guided Beau along the length of the fence until they reached the gate. Beau stood like a rock as she leant down and groped for the latch. Her hands closed around the cold, hard links of a metal chain and she groaned. She pictured them riding through the gate two days before. It had been padlocked and Nina had had to jump off McFly and open the lock with a key she'd taken from the pocket of her riding jacket. In her panic she'd forgotten to give the key to Poppy.

"What do we do now?" Poppy cried to Beau. "There's no other way out!" She looked over her shoulder in the direction of the yard, wondering if the electricity cable was already burning through the roof of the hay barn like the glowing tip of a soldering iron scorching through metal. She looked back at the gate. There was no other option.

"We're going to have to jump it, Beau," she told the cob, swinging him around so they could get a decent approach. She had no idea whether Beau was capable of jumping a five bar gate, let alone whether or not she'd be able to stay on bareback. Would he even be able to see the gate in the dark? But they had to try. She kicked him back into a canter and whispered, "Come on boy, you can do this."

Beau's ears were pricked as he cantered towards the gate. Poppy sat quietly, trying to keep her centre of balance in line with Beau's. The cob pushed off from his hind legs and suddenly they were soaring over the gate with centimetres to spare. Both terrified and exhilarated, Poppy leaned forwards, her hands tangled in his long mane. All too soon Beau was landing on the wet ground. Adrenalin was pumping through Poppy's veins and she found herself punching the air. Beau shook his big head and picked up a canter.

"You clever, clever boy," Poppy told him. "Now we need to follow the trees." She squeezed with her right leg and Beau veered left. They thundered on, galloping parallel to the wood. Poppy tried to picture the layout of the land. But she'd been in such a strop the day they'd ridden back through the farm that she'd paid hardly any attention. She had no idea where the bridge was in relation to the trees.

"I'm such an idiot, Beau," she muttered.

They galloped on. Poppy almost lost her balance when Beau swerved to avoid a deer which bounded out of the trees a few feet in front of them. "Hello dear!" she shouted, laughing slightly manically. The deer stopped and watched the girl and horse as they flew past.

There was a maelstrom of noise pulsing through her head. The pounding of the unrelenting rain was melding with the beat of Beau's hooves as he galloped through the mud. On top of this Poppy became aware of another sound. If she was not mistaken it was the roar of rushing water. They must be approaching the river.

"Whoa, Beau. Steady now," she said softly, and the piebald cob slowed his pace to a walk. He was blowing hard and Poppy untangled her right hand from his mane and stroked his neck. The whoosh of the river was getting louder and soon they were standing on its bank. Squinting into the dark, Poppy could just make out the torrent of water as it surged past.

"We need to follow the river to the bridge," she told Beau, and they turned right and continued until they reached the clapper bridge. Built from large slabs of stone resting on a single stone pillar in the middle of the water, the bridge was around two metres wide and six metres long. Poppy remembered Nina telling them as they rode across that it was almost four hundred years old. Beau stopped at the edge of the bridge. Poppy squeezed her legs. He took a step forward, his hoof making a brittle chime as his metal shoe hit the stone slab. He hesitated, his head high as he sniffed the air. Poppy could feel his muscles tense and she squeezed again.

"Just across the bridge and we're almost there!" she shouted over the wind and rain. But Beau stepped backwards, almost unseating Poppy. She clicked her tongue and pushed him on with her heels. "We're running out of time! Come *on* Beau!" she urged.

For a fraction of a second the cob wavered. Poppy seized her chance and kicked again. He pitched forwards onto the bridge.

Beau felt the stone slab move a beat before Poppy did and he tried frantically to backtrack onto solid ground. But the rain-sodden field was too wet, too slippery, for his hooves to gain any purchase. Time stood still as the old stone bridge wobbled for a few terrifying seconds. And then Poppy and Beau were plunging headfirst into the swirling water below.

CHAPTER 17

Nina had watched Poppy and Beau disappear out of the yard hoping she hadn't sent them on a fool's errand. Scarlett stood next to her, gazing into the darkness.

"Do you think they'll be alright? It's pitch black out there. There aren't even any stars. How on earth will they know where they're going?" she fretted.

"Horses can see better in the dark than we can. And Beau knows the way. I trust him with my life. Don't worry, Scarlett. He'll look after her."

Scarlett was unconvinced but said nothing. Nina looked around the yard, assessing the damage. The electricity cable was still convulsing sporadically but there was no sign of fire. She was more worried about the horses. The crashing and banging from their barn could easily be heard over the sound of the wind and rain. Every now and then one would whinny, setting the others off. At least Lydia had calmed down now the thunder had stopped and was crouched beside Frank, her face buried in his tufty mane.

"There must be a way I can get into the barn. I need to settle the horses before they do themselves any damage," Nina said.

But the huge branch blocking the barn door was an impenetrable mass of solid oak wood that was strong enough to build warships from.

"Do you have a chainsaw?" Scarlett asked. "I've watched Dad use ours hundreds of times. It looks easy enough."

Nina shook her head. "There's an old handsaw in the garage. I'll go and find it."

The blade of the saw was riddled with rust. The rain had made the branch slippery and it was almost impossible to get a rhythm going. They worked silently, taking it in turns when the muscles in their arms started burning but after half an hour, when they'd failed to cut even a couple of centimetres through the oak, Scarlett flung the saw on the ground.

"This is pointless," she shouted to Nina over the rain. "Let's hope Poppy's having more luck."

The water was so cold it took Poppy's breath away. She gasped for air, choking as she sucked in a mouthful of muddy river water. The sound of rushing water filled her ears and she fought for breath, her chest heaving. Her hands felt as if they were lashed together by rope and she tried to pull them free from their bindings, panic rising. It was seconds before she realised groggily that the ties were strands of Beau's mane, which were wound around her fingers like seaweed. By some miracle she was still on his back. She gripped tighter as the cob kicked for the riverbank, his head raised above the raging river. Completely disorientated, she had no idea which side they should be heading for. But Beau seemed to know. She could feel his legs moving under the water as the river flowed past. Poppy pictured a duck gliding on a mirror-flat pond, its face serene as its yellow webbed feet paddled furiously below the surface. Nice weather for ducks.

"Get a grip," she muttered. They were drifting downstream and Poppy sensed that Beau was tiring. "You can do it, Beau!" she shouted. "Come on boy, we're nearly there." Beau quickened his kicking. At last, with a herculean effort, he lunged for the riverbank and she cried out with relief as she felt his feet dig into the solid riverbed. He heaved himself out of the water, Poppy still clinging on, and gave an almighty shake that made her teeth rattle.

Beau was trembling beneath her. She ran her hand down his neck. "You brave, brave boy," she whispered. Nina was right. He had the heart of a lion. How had she been so blind? She stared through the gloom in the direction of the farm. A faint light glowed in the distance.

"We're almost there, Beau. Not far now." She squeezed her legs and the cob broke into a steady canter. Poppy's saturated clothes clung to her body and she could still taste the gritty river water. Soon they reached the gate where Poppy had fallen off. For the first time that night luck was on their side. The gate was swinging open and they cantered through. The clatter of Beau's shoes on the concrete farmyard floor was a welcome sound. But the knot of fear had returned to her stomach with a vengeance. What if they were too late? Was fire already sweeping through the barn, obliterating everything in its path?

The light she'd seen from the riverbank was coming from a single overhead lamp in the corrugated steel farm building to her left. The building was full of Friesian cows.

"Hello!" called Poppy. But her voice was drowned out by the plaintive mooing of the cattle. She cleared her throat and tried again. "Hello!" she yelled. "Is there anybody there?"

There was a volley of barking and an elderly man appeared from around the side of the barn, a border collie skulking behind him.

"Are you Bert?" Poppy asked.

"Aye, that's me," said the man, who was ninety if he was a day. He motioned the dog to lie down and slowly crossed the yard to Poppy. "What's up, lass?"

"Nina sent me. You need to call the police. I mean the fire brigade. The oak tree's been struck by lightning and it's fallen down. The horses are trapped in the barn. And the tree's brought the electricity and phone lines down, too," Poppy gabbled.

"The oak tree, you say?" said Bert, his face ponderous.

"Yes, the oak. The horses are trapped." Poppy repeated. "And the electricity cable is sparking. It's about to set fire to the hay barn. We need to phone the fire brigade."

"There's a problem there, lass. Our phone line is down, too."

"Nina said you get a mobile signal here. Do you have a mobile phone?" Poppy asked, realising she'd forgotten to bring one with her. She slid off Beau, hugged him briefly and went to stand in front of Bert.

"Aye, we do. Our Stuart bought it for us in case of emergencies. I expect Eileen will know where it is," he said.

"This *is* an emergency!" shrieked Poppy, finally losing her patience. "Please, we need to be quick!"

"Calm down, lass, I hear you. You'd better follow me," Bert said, heading for the back door of the farmhouse. He let himself in and called up the stairs, "Eileen! Where do you keep the mobile telephone?"

Poppy jiggled from one foot to the other as she waited by the back door. After an age a white-haired woman in a long, cotton nightie and a coral pink polyester dressing gown appeared. Her faded grey eyes widened when she saw Poppy standing on the doorstep.

"What's happened, love?" she asked.

"Nina's oak has been struck by lightning. We need

to call the fire brigade on your mobile phone," Poppy told her. Eileen nodded and disappeared into the kitchen. She re-appeared a moment later with an ancient mobile the size of a brick. She peered at the keypad myopically. "I haven't got my glasses on. Can you see the numbers?"

Poppy grabbed the phone and checked for a signal. Three bars. She dialled 999, her index finger jabbing the keypad frantically, her heart pounding. She held the phone to her ear and listened to the dial tone. There was a click and a woman's voice.

"Which emergency service do you require?"

Poppy took a deep breath and spoke as calmly as she could.

"Fire. We need the fire brigade."

CHAPTER 18

The phone call seemed to galvanise Bert. He found Poppy an empty stable for Beau and they gave the bedraggled cob some hay and water. Eileen joined them in the yard, wearing a worn waterproof jacket over her dressing gown, and the three of them climbed into the front of Bert's Land Rover.

"We'll go across the fields. It'll be quicker," said Bert, turning the ignition.

"We can't," remembered Poppy. "The bridge has been washed away."

"Well I never. They said it would be a bad storm but I can't remember anything like it." He flicked on the windscreen washers, rammed the gearstick into first and the Land Rover bunny-hopped out of the yard. Poppy realised she was shivering. Eileen reached behind her for a blanket.

"Here, wrap this around you. You must be frozen."

"I hope we're not too late," Poppy mumbled, picturing the writhing power cable. "What if the barn has caught fire?"

"Everything will be fine, don't you worry," Eileen reassured her.

Bert saw the fire engine's blue flashing lights in his rear-view mirror before they heard its ear-blasting sirens. He pulled into a layby to let it pass. Moments later a second engine hurtled down the flooded lane towards Oaklands. Bert followed the V-shaped wake pattern left by the truck's huge wheels. Relieved that the fire brigade had taken her seriously, Poppy drummed her fingers on the dashboard as they chugged slowly down the lane. When at last Bert pulled up behind the second fire engine she unclipped her seatbelt and let herself out of the door before the old farmer had even pulled up the handbrake.

Poppy ran past the two fire engines to the gate. It had finally stopped raining and the first blush of dawn was creeping over the horizon, enabling her to see just how much devastation the old oak had caused. One huge bough had splintered the gate like matchwood and the fire crews were forcing their way through the branches to reach the yard. Poppy followed, her eyes on the barn roof. She could see the power cable twitching and jerking but to her relief there was no sign of fire and the barn was still intact. On the other side of the yard Nina and Scarlett had seen the fire engines arrive and were scrambling over branches to reach them, Lydia close behind.

A firefighter in a white helmet strode up to them. After more than twenty years in the fire service, watch manager Mick Goodwin had dealt with the whole gamut of incidents, from motorway pile-ups to house fires. Poppy was immediately reassured by his air of calm competence.

"Is anyone trapped in either of the barns?" he asked Nina.

She shook her head. "No, just the horses. They're in this one," she pointed to the barn behind her. "The other one is filled with hay."

"What about the house? Is anyone inside?"

"No, it's just Lydia, Scarlett and me. We've been outside trying to keep the horses calm. Poppy went to call you."

"Control said the tree brought down a power cable," Mick said, his eyes scanning the yard.

"It's over there, on top of the hay barn. We were terrified it would set the barn on fire," said Nina.

"Not if we can help it," Mick replied cheerfully. "Right, I need you three to stand well clear of the yard. And you," he added, as Poppy joined them, scratches from the oak's branches vivid on her pale face.

The firefighter beckoned one of his crew over and, heads bent, they discussed their plan of attack. Nina ushered the three girls towards the bungalow. Scarlett was holding Lydia's hand, her freckled face serious. "The horses have been terrified. Can you hear McFly crashing about? I'm surprised he hasn't kicked the

AMANDA WILLS

barn down. Nina found an old handsaw in the garage and we've been trying to cut through the branches so we could let them out but it was so blunt it was next to useless." She looked around her. "Where's Beau?"

"I left him at the farm. Bert and Eileen drove me here once we'd called the fire brigade. They're here somewhere." Poppy desperately wanted to tell her friend about the ride to the farm but now wasn't the time. Mick came over and spoke to Nina.

"We've put a call into control to ask the power company to isolate the electrical supply. Our priority now is to rescue the horses. We'll use chainsaws to clear the branches from the barn door and then we'll need your help to lead them to safety. Is there a field we can use?"

Nina nodded. "We'll put them in the top field. They'll be safe there."

"Once the horses are out of the way we'll need to use the jets to damp down the hay barn in case there are any hot spots. The smallest ember can smoulder for days before igniting and the last thing we want is for fire to break out once we've gone," said Mick. He saw the worry on Nina's face. "I'm afraid the hay'll be water-damaged but at least the barn will be safe, and your insurance will cover the loss."

Poppy wondered when Nina had last been able to afford to pay her insurance premiums. Not recently, judging by her resigned expression. "At least the horses are OK," she whispered and Nina gave her a wan smile. "You're right, Poppy. At least the horses

126

are OK."

Soon the sound of neighing was drowned out by the roar of three chainsaws. The firefighters worked quickly and efficiently, cutting through the wide branches like butter and stacking them on a growing pile by the muck heap. Eileen appeared clutching mugs of tea, which Nina and the girls took gratefully. "Look at you, you're all soaked to the skin. Go and change into dry clothes," she scolded, batting away Nina's protests with an impatient wave of her hand. "You'll be no use to anyone with hyperthermia. And look at Lydia, the poor lamb. She's shivering."

By the time they returned in dry clothes the firefighters had cleared enough of a gap for them to open the barn doors and lead the horses to the top field.

"We'll take McFly, Blue and Rusty first, then we'll come back for Willow, Rocky and Topaz. Lydia, you stay here with Eileen," instructed Nina. The firefighters turned off the chainsaws and Poppy, Scarlett and Nina each grabbed a headcollar from the row of hooks inside the barn door. Topaz whinnied when she saw Scarlett. McFly was drenched in sweat, his brown eyes anxious as he paced restlessly around his loose box. Poppy let herself into Blue's box. The Arab mare was jumpy and she talked to her quietly as she put on her headcollar. She pictured Cloud, safe with Chester in the stable they shared at Riverdale, oblivious to the drama at Oaklands. It was impossible to believe she'd be back with him in a few hours.

Nina was struggling to put McFly's headcollar on. Every time she reached up to pass the strap over his ears he shot his head high in the air and wheeled around in a panic. Blue seemed calmer and Poppy tied her up and crossed the barn to McFly's loose box.

"What can I do to help?" she asked Nina, who was dwarfed by the big bay thoroughbred. He was trembling with fear and reminded Poppy of a coiled spring ready to explode. Nina, on the other hand, was totally unfazed. Coping with more than half a ton of panicking horse was second nature to her and Poppy was in awe of her composure.

"Bring Blue over. She might calm him down," Nina replied with a quick smile.

Poppy untied Blue and led her over to McFly. The grey mare whickered quietly, the sound soft, low and reassuring in the high-ceilinged barn. The gelding stopped his pacing and took two cautious steps forwards, extending his neck so he could blow into Blue's nose. Nina stroked his neck, working her way up to his withers, which she kneaded gently, talking to him all the while. McFly's breathing slowed and he dropped his head and took a couple more steps forwards. Nina slipped the headcollar over his head and fastened the strap.

"Good lad," she said, patting his neck. "Let's get you out of here."

Once they'd turned the three horses out in the field they returned for Willow, Rocky and Topaz. Poppy took Willow, marvelling at how calm she was, despite the commotion. Scarlett looked tearful as she smothered Topaz with kisses and Poppy knew her friend would be dreading the moment she had to say goodbye. As she led Willow past Beau's empty box she hoped he didn't think she'd abandoned him. That was too terrible to contemplate, especially after he'd risked his life for her. Then again, she thought fondly, picturing the unconventional piebald cob working his way through half a bale of hay in Bert's stable, as long as he had plenty to eat he'd be absolutely fine. All of a sudden she realised what a big Beau-sized hole he was going to leave in her life and her throat constricted.

"Your Beau is a hero," she told Willow thickly. The little dun mare cocked an ear back to listen. "I spent the entire holiday moaning about him, and tonight he saved my life. I would have drowned if it hadn't been for Beau." The mare gave her a friendly nudge and Poppy sniffed loudly. Nina had already reached the field gate with Rocky and was looking back to see where they were. Poppy rubbed her eyes and led Willow towards them.

"I've been a prize idiot, Willow. An absolute, utter idiot."

CHAPTER 19

The top of an unashamedly gilded sun had appeared over the horizon, turning the dawn sky the same shade of coral pink as Eileen's dressing gown. Four of the firefighters were using their jet hoses to damp down the hay barn while three had picked up their chainsaws again and had started clearing the branches from the five bar gate.

Mick Goodwin looked at his watch. "It's six o'clock. We shouldn't be here much longer."

"Thank you so much for everything." Nina looked shattered. "I don't know what we would have done without you."

"Just doing our job," smiled Mick. "An engineer from the power company is on his way so hopefully you won't be without electricity for too long."

Soon the firefighters were loading their equipment back into their fire engines. They waved at Nina and the girls as they drove away.

"We'll be on our way, too, Nina love," said Eileen.

"Can I come with you and bring Beau home?" asked Poppy. She knew by rights she should be exhausted but adrenalin was still buzzing around her system and she wasn't ready to crash just yet.

"Are you sure, Poppy?" said Nina. "At least you can take his tack with you this time."

"Actually, I'll just take his bridle, thanks. I loved riding him bareback. He was as comfy as an armchair," Poppy grinned. "But we might be a while. The clapper bridge has collapsed into the river so we'll have to go along the lanes."

"The clapper bridge? How on earth did you manage to reach the farm?" said Nina, her eyebrows raised.

"We swam, of course," called Poppy over her shoulder as she headed for the Land Rover, Beau's bridle on her shoulder and her ponytail swinging jauntily.

Beau had demolished the small mountain of hay they'd given him and was dozing in his borrowed stable, his whiskery bottom lip drooping. Poppy rested her elbows on the stable door and watched him sleep. He twitched every now and then and she wondered if he was dreaming about their adventure. She wished with all her heart that she could turn the clock back and start the week over. What would her wise old friend Tory have said?

"Never judge a book by its cover," she whispered. Beau opened his wall eye at the sound of her voice and whickered softly. Poppy smiled, let herself into his stable and wrapped her arms around his neck.

"I'm going to miss you, Beautiful Beau," she said. He nibbled her pocket and she laughed.

"OK, OK, I'll see if I've got any." She reached into her pocket for a packet of Polos but instead found the card the man in the silver saloon had given her the day before. She pulled it out and read the black print.

Dunster and Deakins
Financial Asset Investigation Specialists
'Always happy to help'

"Always happy to help!" cried Poppy, outraged. "Happy to help ruin people's lives, more like. Poor Nina." Poppy tore the card into tiny pieces and shoved them back in her pocket. Beau sighed loudly as he realised that the Polos he'd been hoping for were unlikely to be forthcoming anytime soon. He stood patiently while Poppy slipped on his bridle and led him out of the stable to an old wooden picnic table, which she used as an improvised mounting block.

The dawn chorus was in full voice as Poppy and Beau ambled down the lane towards Oaklands. Poppy wondered whether she ought to tell Nina about the man's visit but decided against it. It was the last thing

Nina needed after the night she'd had. Before long they were turning up the track towards the bungalow. Nina and Scarlett had been busy clearing the pieces of smashed gate and had fashioned a make-do barrier with three jumping poles tied in place with baler twine. Poppy slid off Beau and led him through the narrow gate at the end of Nina's front garden. She found Scarlett sitting on a bale of hay, her face glum.

"What's up?" Poppy said, sitting down beside her. Beau began pulling wisps of hay from the end of the bale.

"Nina's just told me about the business going belly-up. It's awful, Poppy. What's going to happen to the horses?"

"I don't know. But I'm sure they'll all go to good homes," she said, not believing it for a minute.

"Imagine how hard it's going to be for Nina. She hasn't even told Lydia yet. I know I moan about Mum and Dad not having much money, but at least we own the farm. No-one can ever take that away from us. And it's not like it's Nina's fault. She's just been really unlucky. Why does everything have to be so unfair?"

They watched silently as Frank crossed the yard to Beau, greeting him like a long lost brother.

"Where is Nina?" asked Poppy.

"Putting Lydia to bed. She was going to try and have a nap, too. What time's your dad picking us up?"

"Mid-morning, I think. So that gives us a couple of hours at least." Poppy surveyed the yard. The firemen had cleared the biggest branches but the concrete was covered in leaves and twigs, the untidy detritus of the storm. "Shall we have a tidy up?"

"That's a great idea. It'll take my mind off saying goodbye to Topaz. You put Beau and Frank in the field and I'll find a couple of brooms."

They spent the next two hours sweeping the yard and mucking out the loose boxes. They filled hayracks and water buckets and mixed the evening feeds following the list Nina had pinned to the door of the tack room. By the time they'd finished Poppy was light-headed with exhaustion but she smiled with satisfaction as she emptied the wheelbarrow on the muck heap for the last time.

"It'll do Nina good to have a day off. It must be such hard work looking after this place and Lydia all on her own," she said, picking up a broom that she'd left leaning against the wall of the barn.

"It's not going to be for much longer though, is it?" Scarlett replied despondently. "Come on, let's go and find something to eat. I'm starving."

They were halfway across the yard when they heard a car turn into the track.

"Must be my dad," said Poppy, checking her watch. It was almost noon. They walked over to the makeshift gate, expecting to see her dad's blue estate car. Poppy's face fell when she saw the bonnet of a silver saloon bumping down the track towards them. The sun was glinting off the windscreen so she couldn't see the driver's face, but she didn't need to. She knew exactly who he was.

And she had a feeling there was no avoiding him this time.

CHAPTER 20

Poppy fingered the tiny scraps of card in her pocket. "Scarlett, can you go and wake Nina? Tell her the man's come back."

"What man? Poppy, what's going on?"

"It's the debt collector, Scar. I managed to fob him off the other day but this time I don't think he's going to go until he's seen her."

Appalled, Scarlett looked over to the car. The man in the shiny suit let himself out of the driver's side and stretched his back. There was a loud clunk as he swung the door shut. Clipboard in hand, he made his way over to the two girls. Scarlett melted away towards the bungalow and Poppy took a deep breath and greeted him, her hand on the broom handle, her face impassive.

"Mr Dunster? Or is it Mr Deakins? Or perhaps it's neither. Perhaps you're just a gofer sent by the bosses to ruin people's lives?"

Completely wrong-footed, the man gazed around uneasily. Poppy found his discomfort empowering. Suddenly she was enjoying herself.

"So Mr D - you don't mind me calling you that, do you?" she smiled sweetly. "How can I help? I'm *always* happy to help, but then so are you, aren't you?"

"Erm, is Mrs Goddard available?" he asked, clutching his clipboard in front of him like a shield.

"I'm sure she'll be along in a moment. So, tell me, is there much job satisfaction in your line of work?"

"Well, yes, there is. I find it very rewarding, as a matter of fact," he said, looking towards the bungalow nervously.

"Rewarding! You find turning people's lives upside down *rewarding*? I've heard it all now," Poppy fumed.

"Look, I haven't got time to stand here and discuss this with you, young lady. I'll go and see if I can find her myself," the man said, ducking under the top pole. Unfortunately, Scarlett had been distracted when she'd looped the baler twine around the jumping pole and gate post. As he crouched down his back jarred the pole and the knot slipped undone. The heavy pole fell, clouting his head on the way down. Poppy watched, open-mouthed, as the man in the shiny suit collapsed on the floor, knocked out cold.

She was wondering what to do when Nina ran over to them, Scarlett close behind. Scarlett took in shiny suit man lying prostrate on the ground and Poppy standing over him, clutching the broom handle tightly, and her face went white.

"Oh my God, Poppy, have you killed him?" she squawked.

Poppy shot her a bemused look, then realised how it might look to someone stumbling upon the tableau. "No, you twit!" she said. "He banged his head on your pole, actually. Anyway, he's not dead. I can see his chest moving."

Nina was kneeling down, checking his airway and feeling his pulse. She rolled him expertly into the recovery position and gave his shoulder a gentle shake. He groaned, opened his eyes and looked around him in a daze.

"You've had a bump to the head," Nina told him. "Up you get." She held out a hand and he grasped it gratefully. He struggled to his feet, his hand holding the back of his head gingerly. She handed him his clipboard and said in a resigned voice, "We'd better go inside. I'd rather get this over and done with as quickly as possible."

Shiny suit man looked surprised. "You know why I'm here?"

"Of course I do. I don't know who's sent you, but I know what you want. The problem is, I haven't got any left."

The man looked even more bewildered and consulted his clipboard in an effort to hide his confusion. "Any what left?" he asked.

"Money. I haven't got any money left. You'll have to declare me bankrupt to stand a chance of getting a penny."

"I'm sorry Mrs Goddard, but I think you may have confused me with someone else. I don't want your money. I'm from Dunster and Deakins. We're financial asset investigation specialists. I work for the probate research side of the business. My job is to trace living descendants of people who have died intestate."

Nina looked as nonplussed as Poppy felt. What on earth was he talking about? But Scarlett was jumping from one foot to the other, a huge grin spreading across her face as his words sank in.

"I don't believe it," she shouted. "You're an heir hunter, aren't you? Nina, you know what this means, don't you?"

Nina looked from Scarlett to shiny suit man and back again and shook her head. "No, I don't. Will somebody *please* tell me what's going on?"

"Of course. But first, is there somewhere we can sit down? I'm still feeling rather faint," said the man.

Nina nodded. "Follow me."

Soon they were sitting around the kitchen table, mugs of tea in front of them.

"First, let me introduce myself properly. My name is Graham Deakins and I'm a partner in Dunster and Deakins. My particular area of expertise is genealogy, that is the study of family history. Most genealogists trace people's ancestors, but I specialise in tracing people's descendants."

He paused, checking he had everyone's attention. Poppy couldn't work out why Scarlett was still grinning like an idiot. He took a quick sip of tea and continued.

"Every year thousands of people in the UK die without making a will. It's called dying intestate. Often these people leave large amounts of cash or property which, if not claimed by living relatives, goes to the Government.

"Probate detectives - or heir hunters as some people call us - seek out the families of people who have died without leaving a will. Most of the people I trace don't even realise their relatives existed. And it's a double shock when they find out they are entitled to some - or even all - of a long-lost relative's estate."

Graham Deakins took a stripy handkerchief from the top pocket of his jacket and ran it across his brow. "Was your mother's maiden name Winterbottom?" he asked Nina.

Poppy could see that the sudden change of tack had flummoxed her.

"Yes," she replied faintly. "Her name was Margaret Anne Winterbottom. Why?"

"And you're an only child?" he pressed.

"Yes, that's right. So was my mum. But I don't see what that's got to do with anything."

"Your mum wasn't an only child, Mrs Goddard. Before the war your maternal grandmother, that's

Margaret's mother, gave birth to twin boys. One boy, Kenneth, died during the Blitz. He was only two. Six months later his brother Harold was given up for adoption. It seems your grandmother was hospitalised for some kind of breakdown, which isn't surprising after losing a child in such tragic circumstances."

Nina looked numb. "Mum never told me."

"I don't suppose she ever knew. Harold was adopted by a Scottish couple and grew up in Edinburgh. His adoptive father was an engineer who ran a small steelworks on the outskirts of the city. Harold took over the factory when his adoptive father died in the 1970s. It seems he had a head for business and the steelworks made a tidy profit. Harold's adoptive mother died ten years ago at the grand old age of ninety. The couple had no other children and she left everything to her son. Harold - your uncle - never married."

"My uncle?" wondered Nina. "I had no idea. I'd love to meet him."

Graham Deakins' voice was grave. "I'm afraid that's not possible, Mrs Goddard. Harold died last year. He was seventy five. He'd sold the business and had moved to the coast. He spent his retirement playing golf, according to his neighbours. I drove up there two weeks ago to do a bit of fishing about. I looked out his birth certificate, which named your maternal grandparents as his parents. As you know, your grandparents died many years ago and you lost your mother last spring. I could trace no other living relative."

Scarlett had spent the last five minutes jigging around on her chair like a cat on hot bricks. "You do understand what this means, don't you Nina?" she burst out.

But Nina, devastated to have found and lost an uncle in an instant, shook her head dully. Poppy was also none the wiser and looked blankly at her friend.

Scarlett leapt out of her chair and exploded in frustration. "Good grief, you two. Don't you *ever* watch daytime TV?"

CHAPTER 21

Scarlett's auburn hair bobbed vigorously as she talked. "Have you never seen Heir Hunters? It's my mum's favourite programme. I watch it with her if I'm off sick from school. We're always hoping someone will knock on our door one day and tell us we've inherited a fortune from some dotty old great auntie we never knew we had. We're still waiting." Scarlett sat down again, her face beaming. "Don't you see? Unless your Uncle Harold spent all his money on golf clubs, you'll inherit his estate. It'll mean you don't have to sell up after all."

Nina looked to Graham Deakins for confirmation. He nodded, smiling for the first time that day.

"Your young friend is right. I don't want to get your hopes up too high. The estate's not massive, but there's a four bedroomed house to sell plus various stocks and shares. By my calculations the estate is worth at least half a million, after inheritance tax and our fees of course."

"Half a million," Poppy marvelled. "That would be enough to save Oaklands, wouldn't it, Nina?"

Nina looked shell-shocked but her mind was whirring. "Yes, it would. I could pay off the mortgage and all my debts, and have enough of a cushion in the bank to tide me over. Are you absolutely sure about all this?" she asked.

Graham Deakins appeared ruffled at the suggestion that he might be mistaken. "My dear, my research into Harold's family tree has been meticulous. You are indeed the one and only heir, I can assure you of that."

Tears were sliding slowly down Nina's cheeks and she flapped her hands impatiently.

"Happy tears," she assured them, smiling. "I'll be able to buy new hay, repair the damage to the barn, maybe even get a couple more ponies. But the best bit will be phoning the bank to tell them their money's on its way. Lydia will be able to grow up here after all. I can't believe how lucky I've been, all thanks to Harold, an uncle I didn't even know I had."

After a celebratory cup of tea Graham Deakins gathered his clipboard and was on his way.

"To think I had him down as a debt collector," said Nina, as they watched the silver saloon disappear down the track.

"Never judge a book by its cover. Appearances can

be deceptive," said Poppy sagely. An image of Beau, hairy and ungainly, but phenomenally brave and loyal to the last, popped into her head and she swallowed. Her dad would be here any minute and she would have to say goodbye to the cob who had driven her demented and then risked his life for her.

"You said Beau and Frank were your talismans but that they hadn't brought you much luck recently. If Frank hadn't let Beau out of his loose box last night and if Beau hadn't been so brave we'd never have been able to get help so quickly. The barns could easily have burned down, the horses with them," Poppy told Nina as they walked back to the house. "They did bring you luck after all."

The two girls were packing away the last of their things when the doorbell chimed.

"It'll probably be my dad," said Poppy, who didn't know whether to be glad or sorry to see him. She couldn't wait to get home and see Cloud and Chester. She was looking forward to filling Caroline in on the dramas of the last few days. She even missed Charlie, although she'd never admit it to her seven-year-old brother. But she knew she would be leaving a tiny piece of her heart in the Forest of Dean.

"Will I have time to say goodbye to Topaz?" asked Scarlett, her voice wobbly.

Poppy zipped up her suitcase and gave her friend a feeble smile. "Let's go now. I'm sure Dad won't mind."

Scarlett followed her down the hallway and out of the back door. They crossed the yard to the far gate and stopped in front of the jagged trunk of the oak tree.

"It looks brighter out here now, don't you think?" said Scarlett. She was right, thought Poppy. Nina may have loved the towering oak, but the long, low branches of the ancient tree had cast an oppressive shadow over the yard. They leant on the gate and watched the horses grazing. Topaz and Blue stood nose to tail grooming each other. Beau, who had a couple of burrs in his tail and mud stains on his white bits, was dozing in the sun, Frank by his side.

"I'm so glad everything worked out for Nina. It would have been awful if she'd been forced to sell up," Scarlett said.

"It's funny how things usually work out for the best," agreed Poppy, remembering the highs and lows of the past week. "Come on, let's go and say goodbye." She climbed over the gate and stooped to pick a handful of grass.

"Beau," she called softly, and the cob opened his wall eye. When he saw Poppy he whinnied and walked towards her. Poppy held out her hand and he wolfed the grass down greedily before rubbing his face on her jumper, leaving it covered in white hairs. She brushed his long forelock out of his eyes and kissed his hairy nose. He whickered and she laid her face against his.

"I'm sorry I was so wrong about you, Beau," she

told him. "You were the best last night, you really were." Poppy realised she hadn't told anyone how close they'd both been to drowning. She decided then and there that she probably never would. There was no need to worry her dad or Caroline. It was between her and Beau. Realising she didn't have any more treats the cob lost interest and ambled back towards Frank. Smiling, Poppy patted his rump and joined Scarlett at the gate. Her friend's eyes were red.

"OK?" Poppy asked. Scarlett nodded.

Poppy linked arms with her. "Come on, Scar. It's time to go home."

Nina and her dad were loading their bags into the boot of the McKeevers' car when they arrived back in the yard.

"Dad!" shouted Poppy. He swept her into a hug.

"There you are! Nina's been filling me in on everything. It sounds as if it's been quite a week."

"You could say that," grinned Poppy. "I'm going home for a rest!"

But Nina was frowning. "I'm sorry your riding holiday didn't turn out to be much of a prize, Poppy."

"That's OK, Nina. It wasn't your fault. I'll certainly have lots to write about when I do my report on the holiday for Young Rider Magazine."

"You won't mention Mr Deakins and Uncle Harold's inheritance, will you? I don't want Lydia to know we nearly lost Oaklands, so I'd rather we kept that to ourselves."

"Of course not," said Poppy. "It'll be a glowing review of the trekking centre. Hopefully it'll boost bookings."

"Thank-you, Poppy. I really do feel my luck has finally changed. I know it'll always be hard work, but with a bit of money in the bank to tide me over when things are quiet I really think I can make a go of the business." Nina paused, then clapped her hands. "I've had an idea! I'd like to invite you both back for another week at Oaklands in the summer, as a thank you for everything you did last night. Hopefully it won't be quite so action-packed."

"That would be amazing," said Scarlett, suddenly looking more cheerful.

"Are you sure?" Poppy asked.

Nina nodded. "Yes, I'm sure. And you can have the pick of the horses. I'll even let one of you ride McFly if you like."

Scarlett's eyebrows shot skywards as she considered the offer. Poppy didn't have to think twice. Her mind was already made up.

"I'll ride Beau, please Nina," she said, her heart soaring.

Scarlett looked at Poppy in disbelief. Poppy smiled serenely back.

"Lift your chin off the ground, Scarlett," she said briskly. "Why on earth would I want to ride anyone else?"

Three hours later they had dropped Scarlett home

and were turning into the Riverdale drive. Cloud and Chester were grazing in their paddock and they lifted their heads and watched the car as it passed.

"I won't be a minute," Poppy told her dad. She let herself out of the passenger door, ran over to the fence and called. Cloud whinnied and cantered over. Poppy was beaming as she climbed over the post and rail fence, threw her arms around his neck and buried her face in his silver mane.

"Oh Cloud, you wouldn't believe how much I've missed you," she said, breathing in his familiar smell. "It seems as though I've been away for *months*. It's been an amazing week, it really has. But I tell you something," Poppy paused to kiss his nose. "It's good to be home."

ABOUT THE AUTHOR

Amanda Wills was born in Singapore and grew up in the Kent countryside surrounded by a menagerie of animals including four horses, three cats, a dog and numerous sheep, rabbits and chickens.

She worked as a journalist for more than 20 years and is now a police press officer.

Three years ago Amanda combined her love of writing with her passion for horses and began writing pony fiction. Her first novel, The Lost Pony of Riverdale, was published in 2013. The sequel, Against all Hope, followed in the summer of 2014 and the third in the series, Into the Storm, was published in January 2015.

The Riverdale Stories are currently being translated into Norwegian, Swedish and Finnish.

Find out more at www.amandawills.co.uk or like The Riverdale Stories on Facebook.

16152223R00088

Printed in Great Britain
by Amazon